ASHES

A GRACED STORY

MORE BY AMANDA PILLAR

Immortal Vices and Virtues
Haunt Me

The Heaven's Heart Series
Deadly Passion
Benevolent Passion
Winged Passion
Ascending Passion
Secret Passion (coming soon)

The Graced Series
Graced
Captive
Survivor
Bitten
Ashes
Freedom
Chosen (coming soon)

The Moonlit Hills series
Winter's Curse

The Graced Series

ASHES

A GRACED STORY

AMANDA PILLAR

Published by Maatkare Books
www.amandapillar.com

Editor: Pete Kempshall

ISBN: 978-0-6480295-4-0

Cover Design: Ljiljana Romanovic © 2017
Internal Layout: Amanda Pillar © 2017

First Published July 2017

To Sarah B. *This* one's for you

Prologue

50 years ago...

"Death is coming."

Nick sat still as a marble statue at the wooden table in their tiny living area. As a rule, he wasn't prone to dramatic statements, but that was about as dramatic as you could get. Still, Aria had learned that Nick didn't say anything without thinking about it a lot first.

In fact, he barely spoke at all.

"What do you mean?"

Nick turned his pale pink eyes on her, and her gut dropped. His gaze was sad. Old. Like he'd experienced far too much of what the world had to offer, and was damaged by it.

What has he seen now?

Nick, and their other brother, Xavier, were albinos. In their world, that was a rarity. Most albino children were killed outright. Even at ten years of age, Ari knew they were lucky to still be alive.

Her, even more so.

"You and Xave have to leave. Now." Nick stood, and pushed her toward the door of their small hut.

"What? No." She dug her heels into the packed-dirt floor. The mud-plaster walls often felt claustrophobic, but they were home. She didn't want to go anywhere.

"You have to go. Get Xave."

She crossed her arms. "No."

"They will kill you if you don't go."

"Who?" Someone always seemed to want to kill them. Plus, they were triplets. They stayed together, with Mama. "And what about you?"

Those eyes went blank, like he wasn't in the room with her anymore. And he probably wasn't. Xave and Nick, they weren't like her. Identical twins, they were plagued by visions of the future. Whereas she was just a freak. A real, bona fide freak.

The door slammed open behind them, and then Mama was there, panting, covered in sweat, like she'd been running. Xave was behind her, his eyes wild, not remote like Nick's. "We have to go, *now*."

Tears streaked Mama's cheeks. She took Ari's face between gentle hands. "You need to go with Xave. Leave here, and *never* come back, you understand?"

"Mama, what is going on?"

Xave was throwing gear into two canvas satchels. Ari saw her favorite shirt disappear into one of them.

"The pack have decided to hunt us. They will be here within the hour. We are going to split into two groups: you and Xave, me and Nick. You run hard and you run fast."

But— "The pack?"

Mama nodded, strands of her honey-colored hair sticking to her sweaty forehead. "Go now."

"We should go together." But Mama took the satchel that Xave had packed, put it on Ari, and propelled her out the door.

"*Run.*"

And she did, the forest thick around her. The smells were comforting: pine and oak, orchards, and cattle – the pack's stock. She wanted to go back, to hide with Mama and Nick, but she'd learned not to disobey her mother. Mama was soft and kind, except when Ari or the boys were naughty, and then she got mad. And that wasn't good.

Xave kept pace, barely. Ari slowed down a little. She was super-fast, but while Xave smelled like a wolf, he couldn't shift, so he didn't quite have their speed. Every now and then, he would make them hide, and they'd hear growls and pants pass by whatever dark hole they'd crawled into. But the pack never found them.

Once, Ari heard a scream, high and long and pained.

"They'll be fine," Xave said, as if reading her thoughts.

But she knew he was lying.

"Where are we going?"

"To Father."

How'd Xave know who Father was? Mama had never told them. "Where?"

"It's a long way away. But he will protect us."

"He doesn't even know about us. Mama said."

Xave didn't respond. Instead, they ran and they ran and they ran.

And Ari never did see Mama or Nick again.

***

Sebastian Tailen stared at the remnants of his pack. At least half of them were lying scattered over a grass meadow in the center of the pack's little town, the stench of rot already beginning to set in. Blood and entrails draped over torn limbs, and some bodies had been ripped apart: a leg here, an arm way over there.

He'd been gone four days. Just four fucking days. And chaos had erupted.

"What the fuck happened?" he asked, turning to Irvin. He'd found the old were tied up in the slaughterhouse, alongside two other pack members.

"They wanted to kill the pups."

Sebastian wasn't stupid enough to ask which pups. There were only three who'd ever been at risk. It's why he'd stepped up, become alpha. To protect their right to live.

"But why are so many dead?"

"Lyla. Never get between a bitch and her young." Irvin's lip curled. "They got what they deserved."

"But this—" He waved a hand.

"She was fourth generation."

So much power, so old. From somewhere on the field of death came a wet cough. Sebastian hadn't thought there anyone was alive; he ran to the sound and crouched down.

Lyla.

She was covered in blood, but most of it wasn't hers, by the scent of it. She was curled protectively around a small figure, the white skin and hair marking it as one of her pups. The boy's eyes were shut, and his chest didn't move. Long thin slices covered his body, and there was a stab wound over his heart.

Sebastian's gut clenched. *To hurt a pup…*

A soft whisper. Leaning down, Sebastian placed his ear close to her mouth.

"Ashes to ashes…"

"Lyla, what happened?"

She turned dull yellow eyes on him. The pain in them slicing through him. "They wanted to kill the babies. I couldn't let them. But Nick, he knew. He saw it. He bought them time to get away. I did what I could."

She'd been more than strong enough to be alpha, if the carnage around him was any indication of her true power. It made him nervous, knowing this brutality had been lurking within his pack for years, and them none the wiser. But he would never have hurt her, or any of her babies.

He leaned forward again, voice projecting a calm he didn't feel. "Where are Aria and Xavier?"

Lyla shut her eyes, blood leaking from her mouth. "Gone to their father." And then she turned inward, clutching the dead boy – Nick – close to her chest. Holding him safe, even in death.

Then over and over again, she murmured, "Ashes to ashes…"

Dust to dust.

CHAPTER ONE

Present Day, Skarva City

Someone was following her.

Ari pretended that she hadn't detected the shadow, pulling her navy-blue cloak up higher over her head. Why someone would be trailing her, she didn't know, but she wasn't about to stop and ask them why.

Ducking down a stone-lined alley, she hurried her steps. The passage stank of refuse, horses, and other gross things. Not that horses smelled bad, but their little…deposits sure did. Buildings soared high overhead, limiting the moonlight that crept into the narrow space, their windows lit with a dull, flickering yellow. Candlelight: this area of town couldn't afford the more expensive gas lamps. It meant there was no street lighting, which was bad for the humans that lived here, but good for her.

Part of her almost felt sorry for the mortals who called this part of town home; they were easy prey. Not all vampires were willing to ask for permission before draining a human of blood. Sure, there were laws about that kind of thing, but when a human was high on vampire saliva, they were unlikely to remember if they'd said yay or nay. Even less likely if they were dead. But if you chose to live in a vampire-run city, then those were the risks you took.

She couldn't smell the species of the person trailing her; they were downwind, and there was the whole alley-stench thing going on, as well. It could have been anyone following her, and when you were the daughter of one of the four rulers of Skarva, that was dangerous.

Although, Ari preferred to think of it as interesting.

Ducking into a darkened stoop – eww, the urine smell was potent – she waited to see if the person would stroll by, but the footsteps had stopped. Whoever it was, they were keen on staying incognito.

Normally, she might turn the tables and stalk *them*, but she was on a deadline. Her father was due back in thirty minutes, and she was supposed to have been home at the estate all night. Reading.

Ha.

More than sixty years old, and treated like a recalcitrant child. Probably because whenever she was near her father, she acted like one. They didn't get along. That was probably the best – aka nicest – way to describe their relationship.

Pulling out her gold pocket watch, she checked the time. She was going to have to hurry. Ah, well. She'd had a good night. Peering out from the protection of the recessed doorway, she saw no one – her stalker was *good* – and decided that if they knew enough to follow her, they probably had heard the rumors that she was fast.

With a burst of speed, she ducked out into the alleyway, the cobbles slippery under her feet. It had rained during the night, but then, it always rained here – at least, that's what it felt like. Skarva was a damp place, especially compared to the forests where she'd spent the first decade of her life.

But better not to think of that.

Righting herself on the pavement, she leapt straight up onto the rooftop of a two-story dwelling. *Have fun following me now*. Now she was out of sight, presumably, she started running. Even if her stalker was a vampire, they'd struggle to keep up; she made weres look slow. Suffice to say, there was no way a human could even try to match her pace.

Just to make sure she lost her tail, Ari chose to duck through the Duchess of Roses' estate. It was way too easy to break into the townhouse. A picked lock, a shimmy up a wall, another picked lock, and voilà! She was in.

She doubted her father knew of her breaking and entering skills, and she was happy to keep him ignorant of such. But she needed the practice, and this was the second-closest vampire holding to her father's. Better to have her tail get lost here, rather than in the Duchess of Ravens' estate, which was technically closer. While that particular vampire was apparently on a holiday in the city of Pinton, Ari wasn't about to take a chance on her being home. Ari didn't want her stalker turned into mincemeat.

Literally. The Duchess of Ravens was nuts. Like, rip-your-throat-out-and-then-invite-you-to-dinner-afterward nuts.

But even if the Duchess of Roses' bloodlust paled in comparison to the genocidal mania of the Duchess of Ravens, she was still murderous, and it wouldn't be good if Ari was caught wandering in the estate. Time to get a move on. She skulked down an over-decorated hallway, before slipping into the library and froze.

"Oh, harder, *harder!*"

Nope.

A million times nope.

The Duchess of Roses' daughter and a servant were getting kinky right there, surrounded by hundreds of tomes. Ari hadn't thought a body could bend that way, but apparently... She winced and backed away fast. The Duchess of Roses' daughter wasn't good people. Like, torture-kittens-for-fun kind of people. And Ari could see the woman's sex life was heading in that same direction. Her lover was bleeding all over and she wasn't sure the human spine could recover from that kind of angle.

Wondering if she could bleach her eyes clean, she quickly exited the library before anyone realized she'd ever been inside.

Those poor books.

That poor man.

Although, he might have chosen the...fun time. Who knew? It certainly wasn't Ari's place to interfere. But now she had some interesting information she might be able to pursue. How many of those lovers had survived? She'd be making a few notes in her little black book when she arrived home.

Hurrying down the hallway, Ari snuck out of a side door and into the gardens. *This* was what made the duchess' estate special. The heady and overpowering scent of roses filled the air, making it hard for Ari to pick out the guards that might be lurking in the foliage. The flowers were beautiful – she was tempted to steal one or fifty, but it would give away the fact that she'd been out and about.

Running through the garden, she headed straight for the perimeter wall, leaping over it with ease. Quickly she wove her way through the streets, sometimes over the rooftops of buildings, and a few minutes later she was home. Well, as much of a home as someone like her might have.

The walls of the Duke of Ashes' town estate soared much higher than that of the Duchess of Roses' or Ravens', and inside there were fewer gardens and more work areas. Her father was interested primarily in industry, not beauty.

Scaling the boundary, Ari stilled. A figure was sneaking through the courtyard. She sniffed…and almost fell from the top of the stone wall. That *scent*.

It was utterly delicious.

She'd never detected anything like it before in her life, which meant that there was a stranger wandering around the estate. That was unacceptable: only Ari was allowed to go skulking about town, sticking her nose into other peoples' business. Reciprocity of that nature was unwelcome.

As silent as she could be, she climbed down the

wall and approached the stranger. She breathed through her mouth, so the caramel and fig aroma of the newcomer didn't distract her. Closer, she could see the figure's broad shoulders and height marked the spy as male, and there was a faint smell of wolf on the air. Her own wolf scratched, wanting out.

Not now.

She didn't have time for that; she just hoped her own beast stayed put, *inside* her skin.

The unknown were tensed to leap up a wall to the inner courtyard, and that's when she *moved*.

Jumping on his back, she used the power of her strike to force him to the ground. He hit the compacted earth with a thud, her knees pressed into his lower spine, her hands on his upper back. She quickly pulled one of his arms behind him, wrenching his shoulder.

It wasn't the same person who was tailing her, she'd put money on that. There was no way they could have beaten her back home, and while they'd been impressive in their ability to stay hidden, she doubted they'd have made it into her father's estate. And there was his scent. If she'd got even the remotest whiff of it before...no, it was a completely different person.

So why were there two people acting shady tonight? Aside from herself, of course.

The were twisted under her to throw her off, but she didn't budge. She was a *lot* stronger than she looked.

"Who are you and what do you want?" she growled.

CHAPTER TWO

Sebastian had been pinned rather effectively, and from the weight of it, by a rather small person. It was a tad humiliating, what with him being a six-foot-four-inch-tall werewolf who was packed solidly with muscle. There weren't all that many people who would attack someone like him.

Especially not if they knew he was an alpha.

Those knees pressed hard into his back, right on his kidneys, and his shoulder was screaming at him, like it was on the verge of popping right out of its socket. What's more, his cheek was grazed by its impact with the ground: it stung. It was a good thing that, as a were, he could heal pretty much any wound, otherwise he'd be worried right about now.

A low but feminine voice growled in his ear. "Who are you and what do you want?"

He took a deep breath, to get a lock on her scent, but there was nothing. Night air, coal smoke, and the estate, which had the tang of blacksmiths, leather and old sweat, but the woman herself was invisible to his wolf's nose. Which was impossible. *Everyone* had a unique perfume.

"Name's Sebastian." He figured it couldn't hurt, admitting who he was. He had been invited to visit the estate, after all.

Just not tonight.

Tonight? Well, he'd been doing a little reconnaissance, working out why he – an alpha werewolf with no pack – had been invited to a vampire estate. The two did not normally mix, especially when the were had his reputation. Besides, the Duke of Ashes wasn't known to be a very welcoming sort of vampire.

"Sebastian what?" She was a suspicious little thing. He liked that about her.

How had she masked her scent?

"Fair's fair. You haven't told me your name yet."

"You're the one skulking around this estate, not me."

Suspicious *and* pragmatic. What a combination. Unfortunately, he liked women with bite.

You don't like her, you don't even know her.

Well, that was a blow. His mind was always the party pooper.

He contorted to look at her over his shoulder, but couldn't quite crane his neck to the right angle. From what he could see, her face was cloaked by some kind of hood. "I was just having a look around."

"Why?"

"Thinking about moving into the neighborhood."

"Right. There's plenty of ways you can scope the city out, and none of them include sneaking through the Duke of Ashes' estate. You *do* know what happens to foreign weres who visit vampire estates uninvited?"

"Ah, but you presume that I was not invited."

"I would have known."

"Would you, little lady?"

"*Little lady*?"

Maybe he'd made a mistake with that one. She certainly seemed to think so. The next thing he knew, he was on his back, head being banged against the pavement hard. His ears rang.

Had that really been necessary?

Then she was leaning down over him, but no longer pinning him to the ground. *That's confident of her. Or foolhardy.*

One bright violet eye peered at him, the other hidden by an eye-patch. *A vampire with an eye-patch?* It was rare for a leech to have an injury they couldn't recover from. They were like weres – if it was a physical injury not caused by silver, or wood in a vampire's case, then it could be healed. Perhaps she had a birth defect?

But the extra-odd thing was that she didn't smell like a leech; no icy-cool stench of blood. Yet she was definitely a vamp – yellow eyes were for weres, purple for vampires, with humans taking the other colors.

He studied her, learning as much as possible about his attacker. From what he could see under the hood, her face was fine-boned and pretty, with full lips and a pointy chin. Too pointy; it made him think of stubbornness. Her hair was covered, and her body was largely obscured by the cloak, but she was petite, dainty like a dandelion.

Then, as he examined her, she whispered a word, a shocked, broken sound.

"Alpha?"

She backed away fast, almost tripping over, her visible eye sparkling with recognition. Sebastian didn't remember her, though, and he should have; he wasn't old enough yet that he'd forget a face like hers.

He sat up, the gravel crunching beneath him, the grazes on his cheek and chin healing as he moved. Narrowing his gaze on her, he focused her features, but there was nothing...except maybe something familiar about the shape of her face.

"What's your name?" he asked.

"Like you don't know."

"Would I ask if I did?"

Throwing back the hood on her cloak, she tilted her chin in challenge. The moon glowed behind her, casting the night in silvery relief; the empty blacksmiths, the packed earth, the piles of unprocessed metal. And her. Her long hair was tied back in a braid, the honey color glimmering, and her face was bathed in soft shadow.

She removed her eye-patch.

Sebastian's heartbeat stuttered, then restarted with a kick that had him gasping.

Her mouth twisted cruelly. "How many children has your pack turned on? Too many to remember?"

Her mismatched stare bore through him. One violet eye, one yellow eye. The perfect vampire-were hybrid. The child that should never have existed.

The child his pack had decided was an abomination.

Her brothers, the two albino boys, had been bad enough. There was an unwritten law for weres and vampires that albino children had to be put down at birth. Sebastian's father hadn't agreed with that, and neither had he: they'd fought the pack against it. There was no law about a were-vampire hybrid, but that was simply because there'd never *been* one before. The pack hadn't cared either way; they'd just wanted all the pups destroyed.

The superstitious idiots had thought they'd bring bad luck.

It had been a bunch of nonsense.

"No," he said, answering her question at last, "there have been no others."

"I seriously doubt that."

Even after all these years, there was no question in Sebastian's mind that this was Lyla's girl – her accusations notwithstanding. She'd survived. But where was her brother, Xavier? He'd thought both children had died years ago, lost in the wilds. He'd searched for them for months, after he'd meted out justice to the rest of the traitors, but there'd been no sign of them.

Sebastian should have known better, though. Lyla was their mother, and she'd been tough as nails.

"You escaped *here*? To a vampire-run town?"

She drew herself up, folding her arms across her chest. "What, you're sorry I managed to survive?"

"No!" A pause. "No, I looked for you."

"Sure you did. To finish the job, no doubt." She

hissed, actually hissed, like a pissed-off cat. Then the skin on her face rippled, fur sprouting then disappearing, like her wolf wanted to come out. Probably to rip his face off.

He deserved it.

Not that he'd had anything to do with the attack, but he'd been alpha. It had been his job to protect his pack – all of its members. And those children especially so; they'd been defenseless.

He shook his head. This was pointless. He doubted she'd ever believe him; the pack supposedly followed the alpha, and her brother and mother had died. He'd buried them himself, hands raw and bleeding from digging so many graves.

He held his palms out to show he wasn't going to do anything violent, and stood slowly. "I wasn't involved in the attack."

She followed his movements, her eyes wary. "No, you were just conveniently away."

"Convenient for *them*."

Her eyes flashed. "Packs don't do anything without their alpha's go-ahead."

"I call bullshit on that."

"Really? Then you were such a poor alpha that they turned on you? Thing is, you're still here. If they rejected you, you'd be dead."

She had a point, even though she was wrong.

Sebastian shook his head. "When a pack rejects their alpha, they usually have a new alpha ready to step into the void. That's what happened with my father, when you were born. Some of the elders of the pack called for your immediate execution. My father protested."

It had been one of the worst moments in his life. He'd been thirty, barely out of leading strings for a werewolf. His father had been challenged by one of their new pack-members, a former loner, who'd been just under six foot in height, and mean as pissed-off bear. They'd fought. To the death.

His father's.

There'd been blood everywhere. His father had battled long and hard, but the other man had been younger and, it turned out, just that little bit stronger. Sebastian had been forced to watch as the newcomer had torn off the former alpha's head. No were could heal from that kind of an injury.

And then the new alpha had ordered Lyla and the triplets killed; his second decree had been that Sebastian be exiled. Most of the pack had been averse to the barked commands, but the alpha's will was law. It was the only way a pack could function. If you didn't agree, you left, and no one had wanted to follow Sebastian into exile.

So he'd stepped up. Challenged the challenger. And won. He'd been too young to take on the position and, looking back, it was clear his pack hadn't followed him like they would an older, more experienced were. They wouldn't have betrayed him when his back was turned, otherwise. But there'd been no other choice. No one else had been strong enough to take on the alpha.

Apart from Lyla.

How he wished he'd known that back then. She hadn't had the personality to hold a pack together, and she'd been weak from the birth, but she could have taken on the role until Sebastian had grown old enough.

Aria snorted. "So your daddy was a nice guy, but you aren't?"

He couldn't help the low growl of frustration that burst forth. "I didn't order you killed. I was away!"

Her eyes hardened, cold and empty. "You aren't welcome here."

"I was invited."

"Not by me. And I seriously doubt by the duke. Don't come back, or I'll be mounting your pelt on my wall." With that, she turned and melted into the darkness.

He would have laughed at her statement, a tiny five-foot-nothing vampire mount *his* skin on a wall? But he'd felt her strength. She had the power to back her words up. He'd put gold on that.

All the same, he was going to be visiting her sooner than she'd like. With a grin, he climbed the wall and disappeared into the night.

CHAPTER THREE

Ari hurried into her room, slamming the heavy metal door shut behind her. She dropped her cloak onto the floor, where it puddled at her feet. Leaning against the panel, she focused on breathing.

Inhale.

Exhale.

Inhale.

Gargh! She could still detect that amazing caramel and fig scent. She'd never remembered that about him. Why did he have to smell like a tasty treat? Why couldn't someone so horrible stink like shit, or garbage, or something equally gross?

And since when had he gotten handsome? Her memory of him didn't include the crow-black hair, or the tilted yellow eyes, or the bronze skin with full, biteable lips…

He's responsible for your family's deaths.

Her libido didn't seem to care at all about that.

No. Uh uh. She was not going to go there, even in her mind.

"Beware the alpha."

Xave's words were sudden and loud in her head, almost as if he were still in the room with her, not dead these past ten years. Killed, largely, by his own hand.

Shutting her eyes, she thought back to the last thing he'd said to her. Like Nick, Xave had eventually stopped speaking, lost in the visions of the future. Fate was never set in stone, he'd told her once. It was fluid. People made decisions all the time, and sometimes, they made unpredictable choices. It changed things. Shaped their lives in ways that couldn't be foreseen. That meant some things would never come to pass.

Every time Xave had seen her future, she had crossed paths with their former alpha. When she did, her brother had said, it would end in blood and pain and death. For her.

Because killing her family once hadn't been enough.

He didn't kill Nick and Mama. He wasn't there.

No, he'd just left the pack unattended, a pack that had supposedly decided that killing the unnatural siblings had been the only way forward. Oh, she didn't know for certain that Mama and Nick were dead, but Xave had seen it, and Mama had never come looking for them. If she'd survived, she would have. Ari knew that in her bones; she didn't need some horrible mental ability to clue her in on it.

But where was Sebastian getting off, thinking that someone had invited him *here*?

Sharp pain sliced into her. Her hands had shifted

into claws, and they were cutting deep into her thighs. She hadn't even noticed they'd changed. The iron-rich scent of blood flooded her senses.

"Grrr."

Annoyed, she pulled off her torn, blood-stained clothing. The wounds were already closing over. There were certain benefits to being an 'impossible' hybrid.

Ari was the only vampire-were in existence. She'd never known what to call herself: a vampere, or a werepire? She didn't like either one, but there was no other name for one such as herself. She'd have to give it more thought. *Because you've managed to come up with so much in the last few decades.*

There might have been another hybrid, before, way back when the races had first been created, but none that her father knew of since, and he'd been alive a long time. He wasn't as old as the Duchess of Ravens was rumored to be, but he'd seen a number of millennia.

She threw her pants on the 'to be mended' pile. It was embarrassing how many clothes had accumulated there. You'd think, at sixty years of age, she would have mastered the ability to shape-shift. Most weres had it under control before they reached puberty. Not her.

There have to be some side-effects to being so awesome.

Hah. Wasn't she just a comedian?

Still…she *was* faster than most weres or vampires, stronger too, and she healed really quickly. Then there was the other strange quirk – she didn't have any body odor. Most people had a smell to them, like the bloody alpha with his caramel and fig flavor that made her mouth water. Her father reminded her of frozen lemons, with a hint of sugar. People's scents tended to be a blend of their species, and the unique aroma that was just *them*.

Yet she didn't have one.

Xave had teased her that it would mean she'd never find a mate like other weres, who supposedly detected their partners through a psychic sense of smell. No one would be able to find her, because she'd never show up on anyone's register.

As an abomination that shouldn't even exist, it was difficult to think about having a partner, a relationship, or a family. Who'd want to have kids with her? Who knew what she'd give birth to?

That didn't stop her dreaming of having something of her very own, though.

Enough of that.

She had things to do.

Naked, she stood in the center of her room, her skin prickling in the chill, the stone floor cold against her soles. The other bedrooms and guest chambers in the estate had thick handwoven rugs and carpets, but Ari hadn't seen the point for her room. She tended to bleed a little too easily, and it wasn't fair on the servants, forcing them to clean the mess up. She'd do it herself, but it wasn't worth the war with her father – apparently, duke's daughters didn't do menial labor. How little he knew.

Pivoting, she stared at the huge four-poster bed, its sides swathed in sheer white curtains, the mattress covered in a damask quilt. That was about it for the fancy display. Oh, she had tables and chairs, but they were bare wood and metal, all hard angles. She had a window seat with a couple of cushions she'd embroidered, but that was only because she liked to read in the weak sun that streamed through the bubbly panes.

Sighing, she trudged over to the bathroom that adjoined her bedchamber. She'd better wash the blood off before she went to talk to her father about Sebastian Talien's 'invitation'. While she didn't have a scent, her blood still did, and her father would want to know what had happened to her. Admitting she'd accidentally hurt herself would be almost as bad as him finding out she'd been gallivanting over the city.

The bathroom had floor-to-ceiling tiles, all in a beautiful pastel blue that she'd chosen. The bath had been positioned in the middle of the room, and had gold detailing and four proud, clawed feet. While she loved soaking in a bath, she needed to wash fast, so opted for the shower was tucked away in the far corner. She turned on the faucet and waited for the hot water to emerge, then she scrubbed her skin raw.

There was no way her former alpha was coming back to the estate. Xave's warning pounded through her head; she didn't think she could deal with Sebastian again. He was too big, too powerful, too treacherous. And too bloody delicious-smelling.

She had to corner Father before he retired for the evening. It wouldn't be fun, but then again, dealing with the Duke of Ashes never had been.

CHAPTER FOUR

"What do you mean, you *asked* him here?" Ari slammed her palm down on the huge metal desk in her father's study. It dented a little.

Well, too bad. He'd gone and invited her former bloody *alpha* to the estate, without asking her first. It wasn't like she wore an eye-patch for fun; she was deliberately hiding her were nature from the vampires in Skarva. It's what had painted such a large target on her back as a child, after all, so why would her father risk exposing her secret?

The Duke of Ashes, otherwise known as Parker Ash, didn't even frown, just slowly shook his head at her. He was seated behind the desk, his posture ramrod straight, the white plaster walls soaring behind him up to a high, vaulted ceiling. He was always so measured, it made her blood boil.

He was tall, at over six foot five, and all sharp lines, with ash-blond hair that he kept short – that meant daily trims for a vampire. She supposed he was good-looking, since most vampires were, but she thought he was about as interesting as a stick.

Wait, that wasn't a fair comparison to the stick.

Her father's even voice broached the temporary silence. "I honestly fail to see what the problem is. I didn't think I required your permission to invite people to *my* house." Such cold precision in those words.

"You do when it's *him*!"

"Am I to understand you have some problem with him personally?"

And didn't that just shut her up.

He didn't bloody *know?* How could he not know?

Ari opened her mouth to speak, but then snapped it shut. *He didn't know.* She wanted to place the blame on her father's wide shoulders, but that wasn't actually fair. She'd never told him, now she thought about it, about the pack that had slaughtered her family. Sure, he knew it had happened, but neither she nor Xave had been keen on rehashing their past, so they hadn't given names, or a location.

They hadn't wanted to lose the only parent they had left – because even though Ari didn't like her father much, she'd known that he would have gone out and hunted down the pack responsible for his other son's death. Vampires were like that, especially older ones like Parker: children were precious. And Parker hadn't been aware he'd even had children, not until Xave and Ari had shown up on his doorstep. He might not have believed their claim, if not for the fact Ari was the spitting image of his long-dead sister, and Xave had had enough of his father in him that it made the question moot.

So Parker hadn't doubted that they were his children, born of a short-term fling with a were. He hadn't known about them – if he had, he would have come for them, Ari didn't doubt that. Children were rare and prized to long-lived vampires, even freak offspring like her. Maybe that was why Mama had never said anything to him. She hadn't wanted to fight for them.

Ari sighed and sat down. Normally she didn't bother with chairs; she didn't spend a lot of time in the office, mostly because she was too angry to listen to him. Glancing down at her hands, she frowned. Sprinkles of sandy-colored hair rippled across the skin, disappearing almost as quickly as they appeared.

Then, with a calm she didn't feel, she met her father's stare directly. His deep violet eyes were the same hue as her single purple iris. "Sebastian Talien was the alpha of my former pack."

The Duke of Ashes exploded from his seat. The chair fell to the floor, and his heavy desk screeched a few inches toward her. "*What*?"

So, he really didn't know.

"He was away when the attack happened." Ari didn't know why she said that. "But he was the alpha at the time."

Her father took a few deep breaths, reclaiming his renowned calm, then turned and righted his seat. "I see."

"I found him here, last night. He was sniffing around. Father, it is a bad idea to have him here." Her chin jutted out. "Xave said so."

Her father shut his eyes at Xave's name, regret visible across his features. Talking about Xave was the only time she ever saw true emotion from him – aside from his out-of-character outburst before. But then, he had a lot of guilt about his son, didn't he?

"While I don't approve of Sebastian sneaking through the estate – and I will talk to him about that – you need help. And he has a certain reputation, regardless of what Xavier may or may not have said."

"*I* need help?" Ari glared at him.

The duke looked down at her clenched hands, at the fur appearing and reappearing there.

"You can't control the shift. You *need* to learn how. It makes you vulnerable."

How fatherly.

Unfortunately, the bastard was correct.

"What's this about 'a certain reputation', then?" she asked. "That he slaughters innocent children?"

Her father sat down, flicking his coattails behind him as he did so. "Quite the opposite."

"The opposite of a child-slaughterer?" One blonde eyebrow shot skyward.

"That is what I said. It was very difficult to track him down, but he seems to have spent the last fifty years helping at-risk children. He's rumored to have slaughtered an entire pack once, for harming one."

Chills zapped down her spine.

"He killed a pack?"

Those normally emotionless eyes bored into her. "The most I could find out about the incident was that he killed the lot of them, after a child was hurt. And that it was several decades ago."

Could that have been her pack?

No.

Don't be an idiot. He probably started the rumor so that people wouldn't hate him on sight. Although, would they have?

Not when there were rules about albino children. Stupid, horrible, disgusting rules.

CHAPTER FIVE

Sebastian was not excited about visiting the Duke of Ashes' town estate. He was *not*. Maybe if he kept telling himself that, he'd eventually believe it. As much as it pained him to admit it, however, he was keen to see Aria again.

He barely remembered her as a child, just a skinny little urchin with a cap of blonde hair, who'd been thick as thieves with her brothers. He'd spent more time watching his other pack members than actually getting to know the pups he'd killed to protect.

But he was certainly interested in getting to know her better now, which was absurd. Yet there it was. It was a very rare day that someone was able to physically best him, and even rarer when someone left him slack-jawed with surprise. She'd managed to do both, and it made him keen to see what else would happen.

Straightening his collar, he did a quick check in the mirror. He'd do. Starched shirt, black evening suit and no cravat. He tied back his jet hair, then curled it into a bun. He wasn't into fashion, and this was about as fancy as he was going to get. One shift, and his clothes would be ruined anyway.

Turning around, he surveyed his room in the Grumpy Bear Inn. Single bed, built for were proportions, stone walls, wooden floor, and a small table with an ewer and a bowl. His packs were sitting on the floor next to the bed, a tidy pile of leather. That was it. If he didn't come back tonight, there wouldn't be much that Milly, the innkeeper, would have to get rid of. Sebastian figured there should be something depressing about that, but he didn't really care. The impact he left on the world wasn't about objects, it was about the smiles and the laughter of pups whose lives he saved. Well, that's what he hoped, anyway.

Descending the stairway into the main taproom, he breathed in deep. Wolf, bear and herbs. A hint of tobacco. That was it. Nice and clean: a little oasis in the stench of a big city. Only one other patron was in the large room, sitting in a huge brown leather armchair near an almost-dead fire. Her hair was a shock of white, with sections colored blue and green, and small bones and shells woven into the locks. It made him stop and stare, his eyes locked on the back of her head, skin prickling. Could it be?

No.

Not here. Not in a city the size of Skarva. That was asking to be murdered.

Later. He'd look into this later, because while he'd spent the last five decades of his life saving albino children, they weren't exactly common. Born more to weres than humans or vampires, they were still few and far between. And that's if he could get to the families before 'pack justice' was enacted. To find an adult albino in an inn in the middle of Skarva? Unlikely.

He'd kick himself if he didn't learn for sure, but there wasn't time to stop and introduce himself. He'd already cut it fine enough as it was.

He had a date to make.

***

Sebastian knocked on the huge metal doors at the entrance to the Ashes' estate. The building rose three-stories in front of him, the dark stone cold and forbidding, but decorated with beautiful carvings. The long, snaking gravel drive wound away behind him, leading into a small city square, with two large gates barring the entrance from regular visitors. The crest on the metalwork had caught his interest – a sword surrounded by a laurel of thorny rose stems. He had wondered how 'ashes' could be represented stylistically, and he saw that the duke hadn't even tried.

He raised his hand to knock again, but then one of the doors swung inward. A purple-eyed vamp wearing a butler's uniform sneered down his nose at him. "Yes?"

"I am here to see His Grace." The title tasted sour, but such was life. Sebastian hadn't come from a fancy city, with aristos or the like. No, he'd come from a werewolf-run town that served no master aside from the alpha. But the world outside a wolf pack was quite different, so he'd learned, and aristos really hated it when you got their titles wrong.

As if they'd *earned* the respect. It was laughable; being born into something didn't earn you squat. He'd been taught that the hard way.

The butler wasn't moving.

"Did you need me to repeat that?" he asked, a slight growl layering his words.

More of the butler looking down his nose. "Do you have a card?"

"I have an invitation. Which I'm not too sure I should show you, considering it's the duke's personal correspondence."

"Wait here, I shall check if you are expected."

Sebastian stepped past the butler and into the entrance hall. He fought the urge to roll his eyes. As the servant walked up the main stairs, his back stiff, Sebastian headed over to a set of steel benches against the wall near the door. At least he didn't have to worry about someone sneaking up on him from behind.

The foyer was easily half the size of the Grumpy Bear, with high vaulted ceilings and soaring walls. Considering the decorative nature of the outside of the building, the inside was austere. The floor was terrazzo, which had been sealed with a kind of glaze, but there was no carpet, no art on the walls. There were weapons, however. A sword here, an axe there, a dagger or ten all over the place. He wondered if each of the four main Skarvan estates reflected their namesakes. Ashes, Roses, Ravens and Stone.

He had a feeling that last one might be the most boring, but what did he know about rocks?

The butler returned, his pace slow and even as he descended the stairs. "His Grace will see you."

Sebastian stood. "Which way?"

"You will follow me."

They started walking, at a pace only slightly faster than a snail's. What was with the butler? Didn't like weres? Maybe Sebastian's lack of cravat was offensive. Who knew with leeches?

As they crawled up the stairs, he had the feeling that he was being watched, and not the side-eyed glances being given him by the servant. From the way his skin tingled, he had a feeling it was a certain were-vampire hybrid, but he couldn't spot her anywhere, nor scent her. With her lack of body odor, the latter wasn't a surprise.

Eventually they came to a stop outside a black metal door. The servant knocked twice, then pushed it open. "A Sebastian Talien is here to see you, Your Grace."

As if the duke hadn't known that.

Sebastian strode past the servant, straight up to the huge metal desk the duke was seated behind. It had a dent in the center of it, at the front, which was odd; everything else was so precise, even if the large room had little decoration, bar some weapons hanging on racks. One wall of the room, however, was totally dedicated to books, which made his hands itch. He loved to read, but rarely had the opportunity. Books were pricey, and he didn't make much coin doing odd jobs here and there, between trying to locate and save at-risk pups.

"Sebastian Talien. You're a hard man to find." The duke stood and came around the front of the desk. His evening suit made Sebastian's look like a cit's work uniform, but that was the difference between having money and well, not having money.

The duke waved elegantly toward two chairs by a small metal table. A decanter of some dark-colored spirit and two glasses had been set on it.

Sebastian gave a short bow and then followed him to the chairs. "Your Grace, it is a pleasure to meet you."

He was lying through his teeth, but manners were important. He didn't really give two figs about meeting the duke, it was Aria he was keen to see again. He wasn't really sure why the duke wished to see him, though, and that was what had made him agree to meet in the first place.

"I'm sure it is." The duke's face was utterly impassive as he took his seat. Sebastian wasn't sure if there was a fine layer of sarcasm behind the words or not.

Parker Ash had an interesting reputation. Of the four founding members of Skarva, he was probably the most introverted, although the Duke of Stone was rumored to be a bit reclusive at times. Tatiana Romanov, the Duchess of Ravens, was reportedly the oldest of the four, and the most insane, while the Duchess of Roses was meant to be the most lavish. Having never met the other three, he couldn't really say if they merited their reputations, but Ash certainly seemed reserved.

"So, I received your invitation." Sebastian sat down opposite the duke. They were of a height, although the vampire was built on leaner lines. "You said I might be able to help you with a personal matter."

"You're blunt."

Sebastian gave a half-shrug. "I find it keeps things interesting." And brief.

Those deep purple eyes studied him for quite some time. "I have heard that you have been rather heavily involved in saving…disadvantaged children over the past few years."

That had Sebastian sitting back in his chair. It wasn't that he hid his hobby, but he didn't exactly advertise it, either.

"I'd be keen to know what you've heard." Sebastian hooked an ankle over his knee.

"You prefer bluntness, yes?" The duke reached over and poured two glasses of strong-smelling alcohol.

Gee, that would burn his nose right off if he got a whiff of that up close.

"Indeed."

The duke took a small sip and then exhaled. "You track down and find albino children, or children with physical deformities who might be viewed as distasteful by their parents or packs. You then extract the children, rehome them somewhere safe, and keep an eye on them afterward."

That would be a fairly accurate summation of his activities. Sebastian tapped a finger against his raised knee. "But how does this relate to you?"

"Well, I'm not sure it will. First, you have to answer me this: were you involved in the murder of a young boy fifty years ago? He was albino. I believe he was in your former pack."

Suspicions slammed together in Sebastian's mind, and the blood drained from his face. Aria was half-vampire. Her brothers had also been half-vampire, but were albino, so they didn't share her heterochromia. Aria – and maybe Xavier – had fled to the Duke of Ashes after they'd been attacked. Lyla had been an old wolf, and the duke was rumored to be an old vampire. And Aria had been very sure that she could get his invitation to the estate revoked.

Was Aria his daughter?

Was this some form of delayed revenge?

And Lyla's last words…*'ashes to ashes'*. He'd thought she'd been quoting the old human funeral saying, but maybe she'd been trying to tell him where her children had gone.

"I was away when the attack happened." There, that's what he'd told Aria.

"So I've heard." The duke's tone was so dry it made Sebastian thirsty. "But were you involved in it?"

Not that Aria would believe him, but what the heck. He may as well be honest with the duke. It might mean that he could leave the estate largely in one piece.

"No. They planned and…executed it when I was gone. I don't know how Lyla knew of it, but she managed to get two of her three pups out, and fought to the bitter end." He locked stares with the duke.

"She took out more than half the pack. I'd never seen the like."

The duke's mouth tightened. "What of the boy?"

No emotional disturbance regarding Lyla's actions, as far as Sebastian could see. Or regarding her death.

"Nick?" Sebastian shook his head. "She was cradling him when I found them, but he was already gone."

He rubbed his hands together; the memory of blood-slick palms made his skin tingle.

"I dug their graves myself."

CHAPTER SIX

The Duke of Ashes' eyes were haunted. "Was his – Nick's – death...bad?"

The question crystalized Sebastian's theory that the vampire aristo was the triplet's father. Or if not the duke, someone closely related to him. Why else would he care how the boy had died, especially since he hadn't seemed too concerned about the pups' mother? That disregard was unappealing. Just because she'd been a were that didn't make her life any less valuable. She'd been the pups' mother, for blood's sake, and a good one at that. She'd sacrificed herself so that two of her children could live. What more could a parent do for her babes?

"Well?"

Sebastian refocused. He hadn't answered the duke's question. "It looked like a single knife wound to the heart." He didn't mention the dozens of other small cuts.

"So he wasn't in a lot of pain."

"No." If he had been, Sebastian had the feeling

Lyla would have killed the boy herself, to spare him any unnecessary suffering. While Sebastian's heart broke at the thought, he approved of it. Why let someone linger in agony, when there was no hope for survival?

"Praise the blood." Ash shut his eyes for a moment.

Sebastian had never heard that saying before. Maybe it was old-fashioned, like the ashes thing. "The triplets, are they your children?"

The duke took another sip of alcohol, savoring the taste. "What triplets?"

Sebastian was no fool, and he didn't enjoy being treated as one. To get called here, to then meet Aria, and have this roundabout conversation with the duke? Kind of made his patience a little short.

"The boy," he said. "Nick. And his siblings, Aria and Xavier." The vampire's expression betrayed nothing, nor did he say anything in response, but Sebastian wasn't having any of it. "I know you know Aria, because I saw her here last night."

Ash put the glass down. "So you are aware of Aria's...state."

Sebastian fought the urge to fidget. He didn't want to look intimidated by the aristo, because he wasn't. But Aria...something about her made him antsy. "That she is the only vampire-were hybrid in the world? Sure."

"What makes you think I'm her father?"

Because I'm not an idiot, he thought. The duke probably wouldn't appreciate that answer.

He tried for something a little more...diplomatic.

"You asked about Nick's death. Aria lives here."
When no comment came, Sebastian continued. "Lyla
was a were, so the pups' father must have been a
vampire. And here you are, owner of this fine estate,
where one of the triplets happens to live. I can't
imagine too many vampires taking in a half-breed, or
keeping it a secret. If I hadn't known who Aria was, I
would never have guessed she was a hybrid, and I
certainly haven't heard rumors of one in Skarva."

And he'd been listening out for them. Oh, he'd
heard that one of the Skarvan dukes or duchesses had
a 'special' daughter, but she was supposedly more
than two hundred years old. Too old to have been
Aria, and so Sebastian hadn't pursued that gossip any
further.

Still the duke gave no response.

"So you've made every effort to keep her real
identity a secret," Sebastian went on. "Only someone
who cares would do that. So I assume 'father'. Could
be an uncle. Could be another brother, for all I know.
But you're a relative of some kind."

"I could just be a concerned patron," Ash said.

Sebastian rolled his eyes. "And I am the Duke of
Stone."

Silence, then the aristo angled his head in
acknowledgement. "If you were anyone else, I'd kill
you for knowing about my daughter. There is a
reason she wears that eye-patch."

"I gathered as much. But I knew about them when
they were pups."

Another tilt of the head.

"Is she, or Xavier, the reason you asked me here? I know for a fact that she isn't happy I'm around."

"I hadn't known about your…relationship with my children prior to asking you here. Or your shared history." The duke leaned forward. "If I'd been aware of the association, I might have thought twice about extending the invitation. But Aria needs help, and she is not able to get it from me."

Sebastian frowned. "Help?"

"Before I explain further, I just want to say this. If I find out that you *ever* had anything to do with my son's death, I will kill you." The duke sat back a little. "But you don't smell of deception, so I am willing to believe you, for now."

"You can smell lies?" Both of Sebastian's eyebrows shot up. He'd never heard of such a thing before.

"It's how I describe my ability. But only to a very rare few." Ash leaned forward slightly. "You understand?"

Blab about it and die. Yeah, he got it. Suddenly, the large room was a little too tight for comfort. He was an alpha werewolf, sure, but this guy's daughter was stronger than him, and Ashes was an *old* vampire. He had been growing more and more powerful over thousands of years. And the fact this guy could scent a falsehood? Bizarre, but Sebastian believed it.

"I understand."

Ash sat back with a cool smile that didn't reach his eyes. "I'm glad."

CHAPTER SEVEN

What could they have been talking about that took so long?

Her father was meant to do the meet and greet, and then kick the were's ass to the curb.

Ari paced the hallway outside her father's study and glared at the well-dressed servants as they glided by. Normally, she made an effort to be friendly, but they were checking up on her, making sure she didn't have her ear pressed to the door.

If they weren't watching, she would totally be doing that.

The stone-walled space was rather oppressive, and the bare plaster walls boring, but that was her father: he was all about industry and practicality. Beauty without purpose was wasteful, he claimed. Ari liked pretty things. Sue her.

She wanted to rush over and slam the door open, demand to know what they were discussing. Instead, her feet just kept on strolling up and down the hall.

The sounds from within the room suddenly

became clearer – they were heading toward the door. She dashed to the T-intersection at the far end of the hall, and peered back around the corner as Sebastian opened the door. He said something to the duke, then headed towards the staircase, away from Aria.

He didn't even glance over his shoulder. Or look for her in any way at all.

Wait. That shouldn't matter. She didn't *want* him looking for her, because that would imply she wanted to see him again. Which she didn't.

As he disappeared down the hall, her eyes lingered over his broad-shouldered physique, dropping to his butt; the one that should have been kicked out of the estate. But man, he did have a very nice rear end.

What is wrong with you?

Hormones. Hormones was what was wrong with her. Even though she hated to admit it, there was something about black shiny hair, bronze skin and a shapely butt that was appealing to any woman.

There, you're not being a traitor. You're just admiring him the way anyone would admire art.

Yeah. Art. Right.

It turned out that lying to herself wasn't one of her strong points.

***

The Grumpy Bear Inn.

What a name. She rarely ventured near this part of town, mostly because it was a market district and she kept her spying – uh, investigating – restricted to other vampires and wealthy cits. But she'd heard of the inn, and avoided it. Not having a scent tended to upset weres, and upset weres were dangerous.

Sebastian didn't seem to mind.

Yeah, well, it was clear that he was lacking in the brains department.

Ari was here for a reason. Sebastian hadn't even paused on his way out of the estate, just headed down the stairs, out the door, and into the dark streets. She had half been expecting him to sneak around the back, try to enter the estate on the sly. It's what she would have done; but he hadn't. And so she'd followed him.

Now, she stood on Market Street, watching hackneys drive by, their passengers largely comprised of the upper social set. It was halfway through the night – the best time for attending parties – and normally she'd be loitering in the shadows, eavesdropping and gathering blackmail information from the revelers. Not tonight.

Walking around to the side of the building, she studied the windows that faced the mews. A shutter had been thrown open, and the smell of caramel and fig carried down to her. *Found him*, she thought with a smirk.

Quickly, she assessed the side of the building and then scaled the wall. Being nimble, and having claws on demand, was rather helpful at times. The multi-paned glass window was open, and she balanced on the ledge, staring inside.

A large bed took up the center of the room, with a small grouping of satchels on the floor next to it. Her former alpha stood in a doorway that led presumably to a small bathroom. He'd shed his jacket and shoes, and was wearing just a white shirt and slacks. A single candle illuminated the room beyond him.

Silently, Ari climbed through the window and stopped just inside. She willed her claws away, hoping they actually obeyed her command.

"So," she said into the quiet, "what did you talk about with the duke?"

Sebastian let out a yelp that had her grinning. He spun around on the balls of his feet, and settled back when he saw it was her. She wiped the humor from her expression; she didn't want him getting the idea that she might find him amusing. Because she didn't.

"I see you let yourself in."

Ari breathed shallowly. The delicious scent that radiated from the alpha was stronger in here, and she didn't want that clouding her senses. "You left the window open. It was practically an invitation."

"Breaking and entering is a crime, you know, one that I am told is not looked upon favorably by the vampires in this town."

She could *feel* the sarcasm.

"You didn't answer my question." She folded her arms.

"Did you ask one?"

By the blood, she hoped he didn't have a memory issue. That would make things awkward. What things, she had no idea. She shouldn't even be thinking beyond this particular conversation. This would be the last time they dealt with each other. It had to be.

"About what you and the duke spoke about?"

"Oh, that. Your father and I had an interesting chat."

And didn't that make her jaw drop? "He actually admitted he's my father?"

"Why wouldn't he?"

Well, the rest of Skarva knew, but she had wanted Sebastian to remain unaware of her connection to the duke, so that he'd do his business – or get kicked out of the estate, anyway – and then depart. *And look how that worked out.*

She'd only been fooling herself, anyway. All the aristo circles in Skarva knew that the duke's daughter had an eye-patch, and Sebastian had seen her wearing one last night. He would have eventually been able to put two and two together, if he'd stuck around long enough. Which she'd hoped he wouldn't.

Looks like things were continuing to go her way, as usual.

Not.

CHAPTER EIGHT

Sebastian fought to keep the self-satisfied expression from his face. After all, he'd hoped Aria would follow him back to the inn. It's why he hadn't bothered looking for her when he left – he'd sensed her eyes on his back, and that she'd be annoyed at his casual attitude.

Shouldn't you be worried *that she threatened to skin you alive?*

So worried, in fact, that he'd opened his window back at the inn. He'd wanted to make it easier for her to work out which room was his, even though it let the stink of the city in.

He let his eyes rove up and down her body, noting the still unsheathed claws, the eye-patch, her thrown-back hood and braided honey-blonde hair. Did she wear the patch everywhere? Was she annoyed, was that why her claws were still out? Or was she suffering the problem her father had briefly hinted at?

"So, why'd you follow me home?" He leaned a

shoulder against the bathroom door jamb, deliberately looking as calm and relaxed as possible. He even hooked one ankle over another.

Her eye narrowed. Sebastian wished he could see the bright yellow of her other iris.

"I told you not to come back." She took a step forward.

By the blood, she was a dainty thing, but he could feel the strength radiating from her, her sheer willpower. It was intoxicating.

No, it isn't.

Right. It wasn't. She was just Aria, a girl with a chip on her shoulder the size of a continent and a whole lot of anger that he partly didn't, and partly did, deserve.

"Yes, but I had an invitation from your father. It would have been rude not to make my appointment."

Her full lips thinned out into a tight line. "You could have sent your excuses."

"I could have, but I didn't. A person is only as good as their word, and I didn't want to break mine."

Oh, the look on her face. Priceless. The sheer anger as he implied that her word was worth nothing, since his pelt wasn't mounted on her wall.

And there it was. The skin on her hand flickering, fur appearing and then receding. He hadn't ever seen a were with that kind of loss of control. If the animal slipped its leash, it usually resulted in a completely turned limb, or extremity. Or a whole body shift. Not just rippling skin.

"You want me to skin you? Because I will." She waved her clawed hand in the air.

He shrugged. "I have things to do, places to be. Not having to regrow my skin would be a bonus."

A brief tightening of her eyebrows. "Uh, I wasn't implying you'd survive the experience."

He would, though. It just wouldn't be fun. "That would be a shame. I do like living."

She rolled her eye. "Do you ever take anything seriously?"

"Sure."

Ninety-nine percent of the time. Just not with her, apparently.

"So what did my father want to talk about?"

She was persistent, he'd have to give her that. Tonight, she only had two topics of conversation: what had he talked about with her father; and that she wanted to skin him. He wished her attention would turn to something else, like maybe getting naked – *no!* – or telling him everything about her – *wait, almost as bad* – or just having a cup of tea – *that was better, but tea? Really?*

What was wrong with him?

Maybe that she was smart, beautiful, strong, and hot-headed. All the things he liked in a potential lover.

No. Not a potential lover. Do we have to have a talk?

Great. Even his conscience thought he was being an ass.

All right. While he was enjoying riling her with his evasiveness, he didn't want to annoy her so much she left. They needed to talk. That was it. Talk. Nothing else. "He wanted to know if I had anything to do with Nick's death."

Her stare flattened. "So you lied to him."

He stood up straight. "I told him the truth."

"That you ordered the kill?"

"That I had nothing to do with it. That they planned and executed it without me." He fought a wince. That was a bad choice of words.

"Oh, you sound upset that you were left out."

"That's true. Because I would have stopped it, if I'd known."

"Look at you, acting the hero."

"You asked what your father and I talked about, that was it. It's not my fault that you don't like it."

She clenched her fists, then hissed, ever-so-slightly. The scent of blood, iron-rich and heady, burst into the air. She'd cut herself. Without thinking, Sebastian closed the distance between them and grabbed her hands. He forced her fingers open and stared at the cuts.

"Don't touch me," she said, but she didn't snatch her hands away.

"Did you forget your claws were out?" His fingers gentle, he explored the wounds. And boy, was he surprised to *see* the flesh knitting itself back together as he watched. Weres could heal fast, but this was off the scale in terms of speed. Soon, there were just patches of blood smeared on her fingers and palms, the skin as good as new. Not even a faint scar remained.

Her chin jutted. "No."

"So you deliberately cut yourself?"

"No."

He let go of her hands before she could jerk them back, which he figured she'd been about to do. "Do you realize your answers are contradictory?"

"Yes."

It seemed she was down to one-syllable responses. Lucky him. Having a discussion with a brick wall might prove more fruitful. But he was enjoying himself a little too much, despite the conversational angst.

"There was one other thing your father might have mentioned." He strolled around her, pretending to size her up. For what, he let her guess, too busy telling himself *not* to think about how adorable she looked with her eye-patch, snapping eye, and firm mouth. Or how he wanted to untie her braid and thread his fingers through that honey-colored satin.

Think with your head, not your cock.

Trouble was, his head was doing most of the thinking.

She swiveled on the spot, following his movements. "What else did you discuss?"

So, she was back to full sentences.

"How often do you forget your claws are out?"

"Not very."

"Hrm." He tapped his chin.

"It doesn't happen all that often." That was a tad *too* defensive.

"And how often does your skin do that?" He pointed at the back of her hand, at the patches of fur.

She tugged down her sleeve. "Rarely."

More like every day, he thought. That kind of loss of control…

"Do you ever fully shift?"

"What?"

"Do you ever go fully wolf?" He knew she could. Or rather, he knew she had been able to as a child, unlike her brothers. It wasn't uncommon for an albino child born to weres not to be able to shift; if a child had pink eyes, they likely had a different kind of ability, one that had nothing to do with being a were...

"It's none of your business."

So in other words, no, she didn't shift. He frowned. That wasn't good. Weres were as much their animals as they were human. To cage one half of you...Well, that wasn't healthy. It would be like a vampire trying not to drink blood. It was physically necessary for survival.

He had to do something to show her how dangerous her lack of control was – and how harmful it was to trap her wolf.

CHAPTER NINE

Sebastian was looking at her strangely.

His eyes were narrowed, his face serious for once, and he was tapping his foot. It was bad enough being trapped in the room with him, his scent everywhere, and his sheer presence almost overwhelming. It made her a little light-headed, drunk. She didn't know why the fragrance affected her the way it did, or why his good looks registered when she should notice nothing more than his duplicitous heart. But they did, and she didn't like it.

It spoke of a loss of control, and that was something she couldn't ever allow. As it was, her wolf slipped its leash far too frequently for her own personal safety. She couldn't allow it free rein, or others would get hurt.

Although, would hurting Sebastian be a bad thing?

Why did she even bother asking herself that question? *Of course* it wouldn't be. She had promised to mount his pelt on a wall, after all. And from her childhood memory, he had very nice fur: jet-black, with red undertones. She'd enjoy lying on it in front of a fire, while he writhed in pain as his skin regrew.

"I don't see how your turning wolf is a private matter. Weres are pack animals, after all."

"I don't live in a pack."

He rolled his eyes. "No shit. You live with *vampires*."

"Because living with a pack worked out so well for me the last time, didn't it?" He opened his mouth, as if to say something, but she cut him off. "And, I'm *half* vampire, in case you've forgotten."

"How could I forget with that purple eye glaring at me?"

"It will keep glaring until you leave town."

"Don't want to kill me anymore?"

"Of course I do." But even she could hear how the statement lacked the venom of the night before. Was she already relenting? A few soft words and a look of regret and she'd forget what had happened to Mama, to Nick?

No.

She was stronger than that.

They deserved more. Xavier deserved more.

"Prove it." Then Sebastian was right in front of her, moving so fast she barely spotted the movement.

"You want me to rip your head off? Because I'm more than happy to do it." She forced a grin. The thing was, she might threaten to murder him every five minutes, but she hadn't actually ever killed anyone. Until now, she hadn't had the stomach for it.

Blackmail, bribe, bully, pester…yes, she'd done all of those. Even physically hurt a person or twenty. But never kill. It had always felt like a betrayal to her family, because they had died at the hands of others. She hadn't wanted to do that to anyone else's sister, or brother, or parents. She knew the pain all too well. However, she might be able to make an exception to her rule, just for him.

His yellow eyes glowed. "Then do it."

When she didn't move, he gave a low growl and surged forward, his mouth coming down on hers, freezing her in shock, even as her blood began to boil in her veins.

His lips were so soft, like silk, and the hot slide of his tongue against her closed mouth had her heart racing with something more than anger. Surely not? It couldn't be lust. No. Her body wouldn't mutiny like that. When his arms closed around her, something snapped and she jolted out of his hold – but not before she bit down on his wandering, jerk of a tongue.

"Ow!"

The taste of his blood in her mouth was even *worse* than the kiss. Flailing on the spot, arms cartwheeling like a drunk circus performer, she tried to get a grip on her emotions, on reality. But his blood flooded her taste buds, and it was the most delicious thing she'd ever eaten. Better than caramel. Better than figs. Better even than chocolate. She retched, trying to get the flavor out of her mouth.

Now he looked annoyed. "It was not *that* bad."

It wasn't her blood in his mouth, so he wouldn't know. Shit, she could still taste it, and that just made her want *more*. She eyed the artery in his neck like it was the last meal she'd ever eat. And boy, was she *starving*.

What was wrong with her?

"Your fangs are out."

The scent in the room changed, became darker, more sensual, a hint of something overriding his normal aroma. Instantly, she knew what it was, and where it came from.

He wanted her.

Her.

Not just to kiss and torment, but to bed. And no, he wasn't going to have her. No way. Not ever. But her body was reacting, warming, the resistance in her draining, and her...*no.* She wasn't even going to think about what was happening in the downstairs department.

This wasn't right.

Then he was standing next to her again, all bronze skin and tasty, tasty blood. "Also, your fur is out."

Glancing down, she trembled. Her claws were unsheathed, and a thick pelt covered her hands.

"When you get home, shift, if you can. I think that will help you. Your wolf is part of you. If you never let her loose, you'll cripple her, and she'll fight you. It's what's happening now. You lose control, and then she's there, wanting out."

Shock ripped through her. A demonstration, that's what the kiss had been. No matter that it had aroused them both. That, she realized, had been an accidental side-effect. Her gaze flew to his, and she was horrified by the understanding she saw there. So that was why her father had asked him here. To help with her little 'problem'.

Well, no one could help her.

Because she wasn't fixable.

They'd just have to learn that the hard way.

CHAPTER TEN

Subject 2013 had been in the Grumpy Bear Inn for an awfully long time. That puzzled Naomi Castle, because she'd never seen the vampire visit a were before, and she'd been trailing the Duke of Ashes' daughter for long time now...

Of course, Subject 2013 wasn't who she'd actually come to Skarva to find, but that's how things play out sometimes.

Naomi had originally been drawn to the city by a rumor. The Duchess of Ravens had been understood to have a 'special' daughter, with eyes so dark a purple they could be Black. No one had seen the child in years, though, so no one could corroborate the tale.

And Naomi needed verification, because no one – *no one* – had Black eyes.

There was a universal truth in her world: that people with eye colors other than Brown, yellow or purple were different. Very few individuals were meant to know that, of course, that was the whole point of being part of a secret race: the Graced.

The Graced only had three – well, *technically* four – eye colors: Gray, like Naomi, Blue, and Green. Each color dictated what a person could do, because each color reflected their psychic powers. Marcia, Naomi's Blue-eyed sister, was an empath, and Faith, her Green-eyed sibling, was a telepath. Naomi, well, she had telekinesis. There were also Hazels – halfbreeds like her brother Fin – but they didn't really count. They were also largely ignored, provided they didn't develop any psychic powers.

Any color other than that? Well, her ancestors had been wiping out the mutations for generations. It's why albino children, with their Pink eyes, were killed at birth, a command that had been psychically imprinted on people for so long that they just acted on the rule, even if they didn't want to.

Naomi, personally, didn't like the idea of murdering babies: let them grow into adults, and assess the threat then. She didn't exactly agree with the idea of immortal Graceds either, which was what would happen if an albino was born to a were or vampire, but she wasn't about to kill a baby because of it.

She had her own rules.

It didn't matter that she was born to a family of Hunters, and as a Gray, she was meant to follow in her sister Faith's footsteps. She wouldn't kill someone for an accident of birth, and that made her different, even more so considering she was living in a secret society *within* a secret race. And it was why she'd popped her hand up to investigate the rumor of a Black-eyed vampire. Other Hunters would just kill the woman and be done with it, but Naomi had wanted to confirm the information. Then she'd stumbled across Subject 2013, and the puzzle it represented.

"Naomi Castle, what a surprise to find you here."

Naomi stood slowly from her crouch. The tiled rooftop she'd been occupying was no longer empty, and she silently cursed herself for being so inattentive. That she'd allowed herself to be snuck up on was a bad sign.

"Monique."

The woman flicked her long red hair over her shoulder, and placed a hand on her hip. She was wearing all leather, with weapons sheathed everywhere, and she maintained perfect balance on the slightly tilted roof. Her Green eyes flickered with amusement. "What brings you to this corner of the world?"

"I'm on holiday," Naomi replied. She kept her face, and thoughts, blank. She didn't have natural mental defenses like her brother, Fin, but she had spent years living with one of the most powerful Greens in the world. There were few who could match Faith in ability or sheer strength, and Naomi had learned to construct a shield against her. If she could keep her thoughts hidden from Faith, she could keep them hidden from just about anyone.

Too bad it took so much effort.

"Really? Not spying on anyone?"

"Now why would I do a thing like that?"

"I don't know. Have you met your sister?"

Naomi wouldn't be surprised if Faith and

Monique had some kind of rivalry going on. That would just be her luck.

"So, if you're not spying on anyone," Monique continued, "why are you standing on a rooftop with a really lovely view over the Grumpy Bear?"

"Maybe I'm looking for accommodation. For my holiday."

"Pigs might fly."

"Well, I could make one fly if that would make you feel better." It would be too easy.

Monique took a step forward, her hand resting on one of the sheathed blades at her waist. "Just a note. If you *are* following a certain duke's daughter by any chance, stop. She's mine."

Naomi kept her focus on her mental shields; she wasn't wearing an arsenal like the other Graced, but then again, she didn't need to be. Her mind was her weapon. "I didn't know you swung that way."

Monique's mouth tightened in annoyance. "I mean it. Keep away from her."

Something shoved at Naomi's brain, hard. It was blunt-force trauma on a psychic level, but even though she dropped to her knees from the pain of it, it didn't shatter her.

Something trickled down her lips. She licked the moisture away: blood.

Monique crouched next to her, those Green irises burning with enjoyment. "That was but an appetizer of what I will do to you if you get in my way."

Naomi's mind might have been fried, but she still had control of her ability. Shoving out her power, she grabbed hold of the other woman and threw her over the rooftop, slamming her into the back of a redbrick chimney. A sharp crack sounded, but Naomi didn't think it was the other woman's spine or head.

Naomi got to her feet and stumbled toward the other Hunter. Monique was breathing hard, her face pinched with pain, but she was conscious. Naomi leaned down and kept her voice calm and level. "You might be a Green, but I don't have to be within your mental range to snap your scrawny neck. I'd remember that if I were you."

Then slowly, painfully, she headed to the fire escape and climbed down from the roof. Her reconnaissance mission was over for tonight. Her hands were shaking, her limbs like cooked noodles. Worse, her head was scrambled, and she was going to have an epic migraine in an hour or two.

That was the problem with Greens. They always thought they were the most powerful of the Graceds, and they always tried to fuck with you.

It was too bad for them that Naomi could level a city in her sleep.

CHAPTER ELEVEN

Ari scrubbed and scrubbed her skin, trying to wash away Sebastian's smell. The water in the shower had long gone cold, and goosebumps prickled all over her skin, but she feared that his scent was implanted within her nostrils, because she couldn't get rid of it. Her fangs were out, and her mouth watered, like this hunger he'd started was never going to be sated.

Never, because she wasn't going to have anything more to do with him. And she was certainly never, ever, going to sleep with him. Or bite him.

Why is he trying to help me?

Sure, her father must have mentioned something to him about her lack of control, and she was going to talk to Parker Ash about that tomorrow. Talk. Shout. It was all the same. But Sebastian Talien should have just walked straight out of the estate and out of her life, rather than let her follow him, open the window for her, and give her advice.

It was only after their confrontation that she'd realized how easy he'd made it for her to trail him, and that smarted. She'd thought she was so clever tracking him. Oh, she *would* have been able to find him, no problem – it's what she *did* after all – but not so quickly or easily.

Shivering, she turned the faucet off and grabbed a soft blue towel from next to the shower. Drying herself roughly, she worked some heat back into her limbs, then strode into her bedchamber, dropping the towel on the floor. She stood in front of the full-length mirror, her reflection telling a story she didn't want to see.

Patches of fur were manifesting all over her skin, only to disappear just as fast. Added to that, a pain was growing at the back of her eyelids, like something was trying to push its way out from within.

Her wolf.

"I can't let you out." Her voice was a broken whisper in the room. Backing away from the mirror, she bumped into the far stone wall and slid down it to sit naked on the floor. She wrapped her arms tightly around her knees, her feet crossed at the ankles, and buried her face in her arms, her wet hair draping over her like a curtain.

A mournful howl rose in her mind.

Shutting her eyes, she tried to reason with her wolf. But all she felt was pain. Anger. Resentment.

"It's your fault," she said into her arms.

That's why she didn't change anymore – because she blamed her wolf for Xave's death. Oh, it wasn't directly responsible, and Ari had known that Xave had been unhappy, but she'd needed to *run*. If she hadn't gone out, hadn't listened to her wolf, maybe he would still be alive, would have known that he hadn't had to make the choice he did.

But she hadn't realized how bad her brother was, and so she'd shifted and vanished into the woods behind the city. She'd run for hours, chasing small prey, playing with other predators, stayed out until her pads were sore and her limbs shaky, and then she'd made her way back into the estate.

She'd *never* forget what she'd discovered on her return.

Xave had been in his bedchamber, his pale skin glittering in the candlelight. A silver knife protruded obscenely from his chest as he dangled from the ceiling, a noose cutting into his neck. A chair lay broken on the floor underneath his dangling feet.

She'd cut him down, crying, screaming for help. The servants had come running first, then her father. They'd rung for a sawbones, but he was limited in what he could do. A normal vampire or were could heal broken vertebrae without too many issues, but the silver next to Xave's heart had been more problematic. Against all odds, he'd been alive.

She'd sat next to his bed, in another bedroom, away from the memories of what had happened, but he'd refused to look at her.

"Let…me…die."

That's when she'd understood that he hadn't been attacked; it hadn't been their old pack finishing what they'd started all those years ago. He'd tried to commit suicide.

Those three words had been his last request, and

he'd repeated it over and over, as if she'd change her mind the more she heard it. He wasn't allowed to die, though. She wouldn't let him. She'd already lost Mama and Nick; she couldn't bear to lose Xave, too. The duke and Ari had sat by his bedside, waiting for him to heal. Days later, however, Ari and her father had stepped outside to talk. They'd been gone a mere three minutes, long enough for Xave to stab himself in the eye with a pencil.

She'd screamed her throat raw.

Xave had lapsed into a coma after that. A brain injury wouldn't have been beyond the normal ability of a were or vampire to heal, but he hadn't been pureblooded, and wasn't a hybrid like her. He'd just grown paler and withered away with each passing week, until their father couldn't take it anymore.

Ari could never forgive Parker Ash for dealing out his own very specific type of mercy. No matter that Xave appeared to have been desperate for it, it hadn't been their father's choice to make. It had been Ari's.

Xave had been *hers*.

Xave was his own person. He wanted to die. It wasn't up to you to choose for him.

She ignored that rebel thought. Oh, she knew it had broken a part of Parker to kill his son, because it had *ruined* her. But she couldn't forgive him for making the decision to take away her last sibling, no matter that ultimately it might have been what Xave wanted. Ari didn't believe Xave knew what he wanted, though, not really. His mind had been too clouded by visions of the future – he should have been stronger, should have fought it more. Shouldn't have wanted to leave her.

And there it was.

He'd chosen death over staying with her.

Was she such horrible a person that even her brother hadn't wanted to spend any more time with her?

Sebastian's voice rolled through her mind. "When you get home, shift, if you can."

Xave is dead. Even if you never turn wolf again, it won't bring him back.

Keeping her wolf chained *hurt*, but she deserved the pain. She wanted to be punished for being a bad sister, for not being there when her brother needed her the most. For running away, when Mama and Nick died.

"If you never let her out, you'll cripple her, and she'll fight you."

Xave's power had crippled him, and look what had happened. He hadn't been able to live another day with the visions that plagued him. By refusing to shift, had she only crippled herself?

She didn't want to know the answer to that.

The truth hurt, worse because it came from Sebastian. Now Ari wasn't so sure the were was as guilty as she'd believed. Sure, he'd been alpha, but it was true, he hadn't been there the night the pack had turned. They could have gone rogue. If what her father had said was true, most of them were dead, and Sebastian didn't seem to have a pack any more. That was the sign of an alpha who had been wronged.

So why was he trying to assist her now? Atonement? She didn't think so. It was certainly part of that, but not all of it. Maybe deep down, he was actually not a horrible person.

Are you serious? You're actually going to give him the benefit of the doubt? Just because he has a nice scent and tasty blood? And that you liked it when he kissed you?

'Tasty' wasn't even a vaguely accurate adjective to describe his blood, but no, she wasn't going to be swayed by that. Or by how soft his lips were, how sneaky his tongue.

It was because what he'd said was true, and that he seemed to genuinely worry about her control and what it meant. If he'd wanted her and her brothers dead, then he would have finished the job once he'd worked out who she was., but he hadn't even tried to hurt her.

Lifting her head from her arms, she shut her eyes and searched out her wolf. It was there in the corner of her mind, damaged, whimpering. She called it, but her other half refused to come.

She'd truly broken herself.

CHAPTER TWELVE

Sebastian waited in the courtyard of the Ashes' estate, silent and wary. His yellow eyes surveyed the stone courtyard, his ears perked and tail raised in defiance. A wolf in a vampire den. Some would say it took iron balls to be where he was right now, but he didn't care. If he wanted his daughter 'fixed', the duke would have to put up with Sebastian's methods.

He wondered how long it would take Aria to track him down.

Night had fallen, and so the blacksmiths and many of the tradespeople who worked within the estate's walls had finished for the day. Most of the craftsmen were human, and kept to daylight hours, which was unusual, in a vampire-run city. Normally humans were forced to become nocturnal, to please their vampire bosses. It made Ash seem more human, but that wasn't exactly a good thing – not when it came to vampires. They usually had ulterior motives.

Sebastian noticed a slight movement in the darkness by the rear wall. There she was. She was covered by a dark-blue cloak from head to toe, her face obscured by the hood, but he knew it was her: the slight stature of her size, her bearing, and the anger that radiated from her.

She strode across the courtyard with quick, sure steps, halting in front of him. "I thought I made it clear I didn't want to see you again."

He opened his mouth and let his tongue loll out.

Her eyes narrowed. She wore gloves today: to hide her wolf's fight for freedom?

"Coming here in your wolf form just makes it easier for me to skin you."

Sebastian snorted. He might not be wearing his human body at the moment, but that didn't mean he wasn't able to communicate. If she'd grown up in a pack, she would have also learned the unique body language used by wolves. She hadn't been with other wolves in five decades, however, so he doubted she'd be up to speed on the silent lingo. Snorting it was, then.

The hood tilted as she looked up at the quarter moon. "I have things to do. Are you going to loiter here all night?"

He shook his head, then stepped forward and head-butted her.

"What?" But she didn't push him away, or hit him.

He repeated the gesture.

She took a step back and folded her arms over her chest, refusing to either agree or understand. That left him little choice. Shifting from wolf to human and back only took a few seconds, but the sheer agony was overwhelming during the change. Plus, it left you vulnerable, but he didn't think she wanted to kill him. At least not right now.

During the change, some weres screamed, others moaned. Sebastian had spent years learning to make no sound at all. Skin rippled as fur receded, and bones crunched as they re-formed into a different skeletal structure. And then he was human, kneeling on the ground, and naked as the day he was born.

As he rose to his feet, his breath sawed in and out of his chest, but he willed his heartbeat to steady, and soon he was back in control of his body. He could feel her eyes roving over him from underneath that hood. Or her eye. She was probably wearing that eye-patch again.

"Like what you see?" His voice came out more gravelly than expected.

"It's a little…underwhelming."

Underwhelming? Him?

She had to be lying, because there was nothing underwhelming about a six-foot plus were, naked as a jaybird, and rocking an eight-pack, with enough muscles to put a blacksmith to shame. Sebastian wasn't bad looking, and had a body women liked, and he knew it.

"Someone's a liar."

A huff of laughter escaped her. "So why are you here?"

"Did you change into a wolf last night?" He'd given her the day to recover from their little meeting, but he hadn't been able to wait much longer than that.

"None of your business."

"I thought we already discussed that response."

Stony silence.

"Did you shift?"

Her hands moved in a series of agitated gestures. "No."

"Didn't try? Or couldn't."

"Does it matter which?"

He took a step forward, conscious that his…reaction to her would become very noticeable if he didn't keep a tight rein on his impulses. He didn't want her to take umbrage with Little Sebastian, after all. That would just end badly for everyone involved.

He lowered his voice and leaned forward. "It matters."

"I couldn't, okay?" She paced away from him. "It hurt."

"And the gloves?"

She shoved her hood down – yes, she was wearing the patch – and her face was pinched, tight. "The partial shifting has gotten worse."

"Then come with me."

"Come with you?"

"Okay, bad choice of phrase." Considering his undressed state, a *very* unfortunate selection of words. *Stay down, Little Sebastian.* Or should it be *Big Sebastian?* He didn't want to undersell himself. "Run with me."

"Run with you?"

"What are you, a parrot?"

She blinked. Or was it a wink, considering he could only see the one eye?

"Why would I want to do that?"

"I will go running in wolf form. I am an alpha," –

although, he had the suspicion she was, too, she just didn't know it – "and it might help your wolf find the courage to emerge."

It was a long shot, but if she couldn't shift just by willing it, then Aria's wolf needed help to escape the prison of her own mind.

"So I run with you, as I am?"

He nodded.

"I have things to do."

"They can wait."

She shook her head, but he reached out and put a gentle hand on her shoulder. "Unless your task is more important than your health, then it can wait."

Aria stared at him, and then shrugged his hand away, and slipped out of her cloak. "Fine." She gave him a lopsided smile, and something in his heart kicked. "But do try and keep up."

CHAPTER THIRTEEN

They had gone into the woods.

Naomi watched the distant figures blend into the darkness between tall oak trees, and eventually disappear altogether. She could have continued to track them, but the forest was large and dense, and her eyesight wasn't as keen as a vampire's or a were's. Plus, she had to be careful. When a were went hunting, anything that moved was technically fair game; she could accidentally become their prey.

Why is a duke's daughter – a vampire – going out into the forest at night with a were?

Could they be lovers?

It was an odd combination, but she'd heard rumors of such couplings before. Those pairings were, of course, of interest to her family. Any child that might be produced from such a union had the potential to have a new color of iris, be a new type of Graced. Naomi figured the odds of that happening were far slimmer than the production of normal yellow, purple or even Brown eyes, but no one ever asked her.

No, they just wanted her to watch and listen, and then mete out 'justice' to the unfortunates. Too bad she'd broken with tradition. Oh, technically she was still a Hunter, but there were two factions now. One group believed everything different must be killed; the other thought that those who were different should be protected and studied, terminated only if they posed a risk to themselves or the Graced race as a whole.

Some went a little too far with the observation mandate – Naomi had heard of a group of Graced that had held a werebear captive for a century, experimenting on the poor specimen until he managed to escape. Their goal had been to breed an immortal Graced from him. They were all dead now. Many by the were, and others by her sister, Faith.

Deliberately mixing the races was frowned upon, with only one penalty. And her sister, who was normally level-headed and kind, was a zealot on this issue.

Was death too severe? As far as Faith was concerned, the answer was no. But Naomi? Well, for her it would depend on how these race-mixers went about obtaining their goals. Falling in love and having a child that happened to be different? No, they didn't have to die. Capturing a vampire or were and holding them prisoner and then forcibly impregnating them? Death was probably too kind a punishment. Rape was never okay, no matter how it happened or what the motivation. And when it came to working with Greens, they did it on a mental level far too frequently for Naomi's liking. Just because she was Graced, that didn't mean she thought her people were without flaw.

Overall, however, a new type of Graced was something Naomi had no desire to see. Just imagine if someone managed to produce a vampire or were with Gray eyes. What then? With the madness that would surely come with age – they lived for thousands of years, after all – would come trouble. A snap of control, and someone's neck would be broken, or their body shattered. Or down a building would go.

Being a Gray came with a lifetime's curse of obsessive-compulsive behavior. Everything had to be controlled, calm, unexciting, or bad things could happen. Add that to a lifespan of several thousand years? Well, even Naomi could see how that would be a bad idea.

The faint sound of humans brought Naomi's thoughts back to the moment. Maybe the were and vampire had ventured in the other direction to get away from a camp? But who would be out in the woods, when there was a city with lots of cheap accommodation right next door?

Naomi hovered about the leaf-covered ground, her telekinesis floating her forward, more silent than even the trickiest of weres. She blurred the air in front of her, making it hard to lock onto her physical appearance and muddying her scent. Approaching the noises, she found a nice patch of deep shadow on the edge of a small clearing and looked around.

Monique.

And she wasn't alone. There were another four people – two men and two women – in the open expanse, all seated before a fire that burned merrily in the center of a camp. Some small animal was being rotated over the flames on a spit. Two canvas tents had been erected off to the side, and a small pile of gear lay near the fire. A horse was tethered on the opposite side of the clearing, a blanket spread over its back.

Quickly, Naomi made her thoughts as blank as she could, while still trying to listen in to their conversation.

"I think it's the one." Monique leaned over and grabbed a pack from near her feet.

"Are you sure?" This was from a man whose face was largely in shadow, but who had silvered hair. Did Naomi detect a hint of Gray in his eyes?

"No, I was just making it up."

"We have to be sure." This was from a woman who bore a remarkable resemblance to Monique, but an older version. A sister or even her mother?

"It's why I said 'I think', rather than 'I know'."

The other two remained quiet, but Naomi had no doubt they were also Graced. What color eyes did they have? It was hard to tell from her position. Most Hunters were Greens and Grays. Blues struggled with the job – it was difficult to be an assassin when you could feel every emotion your victim was suffering as you killed them.

"Is the brother still alive?"

Brother?

Naomi thought back to what she knew about the

duke's daughter. Yes, there'd been another child, but he'd died long before Naomi had arrived in Skarva. There had been rumors he'd been an albino, but nothing had been confirmed. Naomi had considered that the duke himself might have started the gossip, to give his family an air of mystery – potentially to match that surrounding the Duchess of Ravens and her 'special' child. Now, listening to this, she wondered if the story may well have been true.

It was rare for vampires to have albino offspring, and that just made her all the more suspicious of Subject 2013. It was the eye-patch that had originally caught her attention – and the way the girl moved. She had the speed and agility of someone much older and more powerful, or like someone who had Gray eyes. Or *a* Gray eye. Everyone said that the girl had been injured as a baby, and that her covered eye had been damaged beyond repair. But what if she was hiding heterochromia?

Naomi had been studying her to find out.

"There is no sign of any brother," Monique said. "If he truly was albino, he's probably dead. You know how weres get. Even vampires. Our programming is too effective."

'Programming'. What a nice way to describe deeply implanted mind-control, mind-control so strong it was passed on as a genetic memory. The command didn't work on those with natural mental shields, though, no matter if it was effective on their parents and siblings, but people with that handy talent were supposedly few and far between.

"That leaves only the abomination."

Abomination?

It seemed Naomi's guesses about Subject 2013 had been correct. Hunters wouldn't bother using that kind of language for a normal vampire. They didn't like them, but wouldn't go so far as to label them an 'abomination'.

"I just need to confirm it's truly her, and then I will make the kill," Monique said.

"If you suspect," said one of the previously silent listeners, "kill her anyway."

"She is the daughter of the Duke of Ashes. If we kill her and she isn't the one we're after, he will come after us."

"If she really is his daughter, and he's harbored her here for all those years, he will seek justice anyway," offered Monique's mother/sister/aunt. "Kill her and be done with it. Make it look like an accident."

She'd changed her tune pretty quickly.

"We don't slay innocents."

Hah! That was rich, coming from Monique. She was a straight-out killer. Naomi doubted the woman had ever considered whether her prey was blameless on not – her definition of 'innocent' seemed rather skewed.

"When will you learn? No one is innocent. Especially not a vampire-were hybrid. Kill the girl and then we can leave."

A vampire-were what?

Chapter Fourteen

They'd gone running every night for the past week, and Ari's wolf still refused to emerge. It hung back in the corner of her mind, whining in pain and anger. Even though she was now willing to give it free rein, it just didn't trust her anymore.

Which was a sad state of affairs, considering that her wolf was part of her.

But that was her life: things always went wrong.

Standing under the arched stone entryway into the estate, she felt eyes on her again. She'd had the feeling she was being watched for days, and the only time the sensation lapsed lately was in the estate proper, and in the forest. She had no idea who was following her – they were good – but she was getting mighty sick of their stalking.

Leaning down, she grabbed Sebastian's scruff. His pelt was warm in her hands, the fur ever-so soft. She pushed the sensations from her thoughts.

Her voice quiet, she asked, "Do you smell anything?" Ari's sense of smell was impressive, but she wore her human nose now. In wolf form, Sebastian's might be a bit better right now. Although, if she'd shifted…but that wasn't the case.

The wolf lifted his nose to the air. Reluctantly, she let go of him and stepped back.

A small whine. She took it to be a question.

Crouching down, she murmured, "Someone is following us."

He raised his nose again, and huffed wetly as he took in the air. A small shake of the head. His bright eyes were sad in his sooty face.

"Next time."

Opening the rear door into the estate, she nodded at the vampire guard on duty and headed toward the inner courtyard. Sebastian followed her quietly. Her hand was still hot from where she'd touched him. She'd avoided contact the entire time they'd been making these nightly runs, because she hadn't wanted a repeat of what happened at the inn. Sure, he'd largely been in wolf form tonight, but he'd proven it didn't take long for him to return to his human body.

And that was the body she was most worried about.

Early in the morning, when she'd return from her nightly rounds of the city, she would still smell his scent on her sometimes, taste his blood in her mouth, even though she'd only ever had that tiny sample. It made her body *burn*. She'd never endured that kind of hunger before, and it terrified her with its intensity. She shouldn't want him – couldn't want him, not like that. But she did, and she needed to avoid any contact that could create a spark.

Oblivious to her thoughts, Sebastian followed her quietly as she made her way through the estate. She opened a door, allowing him inside the main building. "Would you like something to eat?"

He shook his head, so Ari led him up the servant's stairway and down the back corridors to her room.

Is it wise to have him in your bedchamber?

No, it wasn't, but she'd stashed his clothes there, and she wanted to talk to him away from prying eyes. If they were in a parlor or a sitting room, her father's servants would be nearby and their eavesdropping habits was almost as bad as hers.

Once inside the room, she motioned to the bathroom. "Your clothes are in there."

Sebastian nodded again and then padded over to the ensuite, nudging the door shut with his head. Weres weren't uncomfortable with nakedness, but she certainly was with his. She hung her cloak on a hook to avoid thinking about his eight-pack, and his broad shoulders, and his amazing butt...

Failed.

Part of her wished that he was affected by her as she was him. She didn't have a scent, however, so there was no way he could react the way she did, every time he came near her. She knew he wasn't attracted to her like that anyway: he always shifted at least once during their runs to command *her* to change, and he never got hard during the process. She'd checked.

Too many times.

Even unaroused, he was something to behold.

Stop right there. You're being a pervert.

There was nothing wrong with looking.

He's trying to help you, but he's still the alpha who let your mother and brother die.

Perhaps she'd imagined the lust that had poured off him back at the inn that time, but she couldn't understand why she'd make something like that up.

"Who do you think is following you?" Sebastian stood in the bathroom doorway, his shirt loosely buttoned, and buckskin pants hanging low, the dark line of hair leading to his waistband visible. She snapped her gaze up to meet his.

"I have no idea." If she knew, she'd be hunting them down.

"You should try and find out."

"No shit." She wasn't exactly free when it came to time, though. She had her evening jaunts of failure with her former alpha, and then there was her spying, which took up the rest of the night. And she needed to sleep. Not a lot, but enough that she had to make time for it.

He changed the topic. "Your wolf should recognize mine as alpha and obey."

She growled, low. Just because he had once been her alpha, that didn't mean that she still recognized him as such. Because she didn't; she had no alpha and was most assuredly a loner.

"Maybe that's the problem," she said. "My wolf trust doesn't you. And doesn't consider you her alpha."

"Your wolf doesn't trust *you*."

She winced. That was no doubt true as well. "You

keep blaming me, but maybe it's partly to do with you."

He took a step toward her. "It's not always my fault."

"I didn't say it was."

"You pretty much did."

She tugged on the end of her braid. "Look, I don't know why my wolf refuses to come out now that I am trying to get her to."

"It's not 'her' versus 'you.' It's *you* versus *you.* Maybe that's part of the problem."

"So now you are saying that it's how I *think*?"

Would she never get a break? Was everything she did wrong?

"Look, you've separated your identities for some reason, but they should act as one. The wolf is you and you are the wolf."

"Maybe that's how it's meant to be for a normal were. But I've never been a normal were."

Wasn't that the truth?

"I've always been different. My wolf has always felt…separate from me. Like we're two halves of a whole. Maybe the best way to think of it is like twins."

Or triplets.

Sebastian frowned. "I guess that could be possible."

"I'm *half vampire.* Of course it's possible. I shouldn't even exist, according to nature."

Although, considering that vampires and weres were rumored to have been created by *humans*, thousands and thousands of years ago, maybe nature didn't have a whole lot to do with anything, anymore.

"We could try with just focusing on small shifts – hands, or feet, or ears – for a little while. See how that goes." Sebastian ran a hand over his hair, which was loose and shiny and ever-so silky-looking.

Argh! What was wrong with her?

"I can make claws." Although not always when she wanted to.

"Yeah, we want a little more than that."

A small silence, then she blurted, "Why are you doing this?"

Oh, she *didn't*.

CHAPTER FIFTEEN

"Why are you doing this?" As soon as the words left her mouth, embarrassment turned her cheeks red.

Sebastian winced; for him and for her. He suspected the answer 'I don't know' wasn't going to be good enough. After all, *he* wasn't exactly sure why he had agreed to help her, either. Oh, there were plenty of reasons – guilt, atonement, the challenge, lust – but when he actually thought about it, they were all too simple.

Just being near her made his body crave her touch, his skin tingle, and his inner wolf go crazy. Every part of him wanted her, and it was a building fire that was going to burn him alive. Her resilience, her mental strength, her physical prowess, even her bloody-mindedness, appealed to him on a deep, primal level.

And the worst part? He knew she could never feel the same way back, for some very strong reasons. He was an idiot, led around by his cock. After all, *how* could he let himself want her? She'd been a child that should have been protected in his pack, but her family was murdered instead. He *owed* her more than a hard-on; he just wished he could convince his body to get onboard with that.

She's not a child any longer, and she's attracted to you.

No, she wasn't.

Why did she kiss you back?

He'd wondered about that. A lot.

"Well?" She was tapping her foot.

He shoved a hand through his hair, then quickly tied it back with a small piece of leather. "It's not right."

"What isn't?" Her stare narrowed.

"That you can't change."

He had to wonder if it was somehow his fault. Oh, she'd been able to fully shift as a child, but had she been able to since she left the pack? He didn't know. It was something he really should have asked earlier, but she wasn't the type to let him ask personal questions.

"Of course it isn't right. That's why I am letting you help me."

"How long has it been since you shifted?"

The flash of pain in her expression pierced him. "Ten years."

So she had been able to shift after she left the pack, which meant it wasn't a lack of other weres that had caused the problem.

"What happened a decade ago?"

"Not going there with you."

Now he was on to something; she only clammed up when it was private. He moved right up into her personal space, but she didn't step back. No, she just tilted her chin up in defiance.

"What happened?" His voice was low.

She has *to be an alpha.*

The truth of it settled into his bones. Alphas were rare – only one was born in maybe every two or three hundred – and considering were birth-rates weren't all that high to begin with…

No other were could tolerate being so close to him without acceding to his dominance. Only another alpha would challenge him back, and she'd been fighting him ever since he walked back into the estate. Maybe half of her dislike of him stemmed from her wolf protecting itself, because two alphas together? A perfect match on paper, a terrible one in reality.

It also explained why she wouldn't shift when he ordered her to. Her wolf wouldn't – or couldn't – recognize his authority.

That red mouth. Blood, he was so close to her now, he could almost taste her lips. Her lack of scent was driving his wolf nuts in a way that just excited him more, because he couldn't tell if she was aroused, enraged or just bored by him. He was also hard as a rock. Thank goodness for his foresight in bringing clothes, because his arousal would be hard to miss, otherwise.

"I'm not telling you."

He leaned down. Her breath smelled of mint. "Yes, you are."

"No."

"I need to know."

"Trust me, you don't."

"Look, I can't help you if I don't know—"

A low growl rose from Aria, and then her lips were on his. They were cool, but plump and silky. He stood there, immobile, stunned. She nibbled gently on his lower lip, and then sucked it into her mouth. Her hand moved up to her face and flicked the eye-patch away. Both eyes opened then, her mismatched stare going straight through him.

His voice hoarse, he asked, "What are you—?"

Then she kissed him again. Harder this time, more demanding. Her tongue thrust into his mouth, and his control shattered, like he'd wanted her forever, no matter that it had only been a week. And now *she* was kissing *him*. His arms wrapped around her, and he hauled her close, every inch of him plastered against her. It wasn't enough.

Her hands were everywhere, stroking over his shoulders and back, and then she hopped up, her legs wrapping around his waist, pressing her sex right against his erection. He pulled away from the kiss with a moan, and then his mouth was moving over her jaw and neck, leaving a trail of desperate kisses. He didn't know who started it, but she was riding him, grinding against him, her hips matching his thrusts. He thought he'd explode, and he wasn't even inside her yet. Their clothes were a barrier he hated, but some small, sane part of his mind said he needed to keep his pants on.

Raising his head, he looked at her: head thrown back, neck exposed, panting, her mouth open to reveal her fangs. She was the most beautiful thing he'd ever seen.

He couldn't stop the words from coming. "Bite me."

Her eyes flew open.

"Bite. Me."

A little breathy moan and then she struck; so fast he couldn't see it. Her fangs pierced his neck, the pain sharp, intense, and then fading as his body healed the damage. She bit him again, sucking against the wound, and it burned, ramping up the pleasure as her hips ground against his cock.

She moaned and turned wild while her mouth latched onto his neck, her body writhing against his. Her claws dug into his back, cutting his skin. She'd lost control, and it just made it better. Sebastian cupped a hand behind her head, pushing her against his neck. She could drink every last drop of his blood, he didn't care, just as long as she kept moving against him, kept her fangs *in* him.

Seconds later, she pulled away, her lips red and glistening, and her whole body tensed. She pressed against him, gasping, whispering his name as she shuddered and came.

Pleasure spiked out of control, his balls going tight, tingles shooting down from his spine, lights exploding behind his eyes. He pumped against her, spilling into his pants like a teenager with his first lover.

It had been the best orgasm of his life.

He held on tight, her body limp and sated in his arms, her defenses down. Right now, he could ask her about her wolf, and she'd probably answer, but he didn't want to ruin what they'd just shared. For this brief moment in time, they had an accord, their bodies in perfect sync. They could deal with all the drama later.

CHAPTER SIXTEEN

What just happened?

Ari's brain wouldn't get back on track; her nerve endings were fried, the pleasure she'd just experienced overriding everything. She could still taste Sebastian's blood on her tongue, and she shivered with remembered ecstasy. His arms were around her, and he was slowly sinking to his knees, gently lowering her with him. Cradling her, like she was a treasure.

One minute she'd been kissing him to shut him up, and the next, she'd been riding him, out of control, her body desperate for release, his blood in her mouth. They technically hadn't even had intercourse, but it was the best sex of her life.

She couldn't imagine how good it would feel to have him inside her.

No. Don't go there.

Those mental warnings were wearing thin: chemistry like they had was rare, even she knew that. But physical lust shouldn't be enough to make her forgive him for her past. For Mama and Nick.

"Aria, I—"

She thrust herself away from him, landing hard on her butt on the stone floor. If Sebastian apologized, she'd splinter. After everything that they'd said and done, this had certainly been bad idea but she couldn't regret it. Not right now, not when aftershocks were *still* making her body sing.

"If you say you're sorry, I will rip your throat out."

He laughed, a low chuckle that had her insides warming in a completely different way. *You're in trouble.*

No shit.

He met her gaze, his expression serious. "Fuck no, I am *not* sorry that just happened."

Relief poured through her, and the intensity of the emotion shocked her. She sat there on the floor in front of her former alpha, raw and exposed. It didn't matter she was still fully clothed, she'd never felt so naked before. Like he could see *her*, all the flaws and secrets and shadows she'd kept caged alongside her wolf for years.

"Then what were you about to say?"

He moved closer to her, and ran a thumb over her lip. "That I should get going soon."

"So you're a bang 'em and leave 'em kinda guy?" Oh no, she didn't just say that. When it came to Sebastian, her mouth had a mind of its own.

He pulled his hand away. "Sometimes. I just didn't think you'd want me to stay."

"Right."

She wasn't sure she believed that excuse, but

maybe him going would be a good thing. It would help get her equilibrium back.

"I can stay if you want?"

She shook her head. "It's okay. You should go. I have things to do." And she did have things to do. She was sure of it. Things that did not involve mooning over the were in front of her. Or worse, actually having sex with the guy. There'd be no going back from that.

He didn't look convinced, but turned toward the bathroom anyway. The back of his shirt was shredded and covered in blood. She'd done that.

"I'm so sorry."

He spun back, mouth compressed into a thin line. "Now who's the one apologizing?"

She pointed. "Your shirt, I shredded it. It's covered in blood. I'm sorry I hurt you."

He strode to her and presented his back, tugging away bits of the shirt. "They've already healed."

And they had. She pressed a trembling finger to a faint pink line that would no doubt vanish within the hour. He was a fast healer. Not as quick as her, but then, no one was.

"But didn't it hurt?"

Just because vampires and weres could heal fast, it didn't mean they were pain-free. They suffered just as much as a human, from what she understood. The injuries just faded faster.

He gently cupped her cheeks and pressed his mouth against hers, soft, fleeting, tender. "It felt fucking amazing."

Ari's cheeks burned.

He disappeared into the bathroom, no doubt to clean up, and emerged soon after, his feet bare, his shirt gone. He gave a shrug when she raised her eyebrows.

"It was past salvaging."

Then he swooped down, pressed another firm kiss to her mouth, and was heading out the door of her chamber. He shot a heavy-lidded glance back at her. "I'll see you tomorrow night."

Then he was gone. She stared at the closed door.

You can't just sit here all night.

No, she had her errands to run. The world tilted a little as she stood up, and it took a second to get her bearings. She righted her clothing and then headed to the far corner of her room. Pressing a stone that looked like all the surrounding others, she waited as the secret panel slid open. Then she retrieved the small leather-bound book that she had stashed there.

Her little black book of names.

Flipping it open to the third-last entry, she nodded to herself. Each name in this book was an influential person in the city of Skarva, and she had dirt on every one of them. She'd started spying long before Xave had hung himself. It had been her attempt at protecting the family, ensuring that anyone who came after her and her brother would regret it. She had enough material to blackmail most people in the city into the next century.

It was amazing how aristos and cits backed down when their livelihood or reputations were on the line. Some had even managed to forget they'd ever seen an albino child near the Duke of Ashes' estate. They'd certainly never come after Xave as a result. Or her. After Xave had gone, she'd kept the habit up, because her life was never going to be safe, and while she hated her father for what he'd done with Xave, he was the only relative she had left.

No one touched what was hers.

Yet somehow, during the last hour, things had changed. Shifted. Now she didn't have just one person to protect, she had two. Sebastian had managed to wrangle his way into her life, and she wasn't sure she could deal with it when he left. And he would leave. But for now, while he was in Skarva, and dealing with her, he was under her protection.

No one would get to kill her former alpha except her.

It was time to go hunting.

CHAPTER SEVENTEEN

Naomi was perched on the high stone wall that ran around the Duke of Ashes' town estate. She wouldn't have dared get this close to her quarry normally, but tonight was an exception.

Monique was here.

The Green and another Hunter were also crouched atop the perimeter wall of the estate, hidden within the shadows. Naomi was invisible to them, thanks to her ability – she had developed a sight-shield as a child, while hiding from two very powerful sisters and one annoying brother – but they were clear as day to her. That meant a vampire would be able to spot them, too.

What were they *doing*?

Minutes later, Subject 2013 emerged from the inner courtyard, striding into the large expanse of the outer yard. Her footsteps, cat-like and graceful, were silent in the night, and a large blue cloak billowed around her. The same garment she wore for concealment gave her away – she wore it everywhere, day and night.

A vampire-were hybrid. Naomi shook her head. She'd known something wasn't right with the woman, but she hadn't considered that possibility. Why would she? There had never been such a thing on record before, and there had no doubt been vampire and were matings previously. The two species hadn't always hated each other.

So Naomi's suspicions had been wrong: Aria Ash's strangeness had had nothing to do with being Graced. The revelation did raise a number of concerns, though. If there was one half-breed, could there be more? And what could they do? Were they as powerful as a normal vampire or were, or more so? Could they shift? Could they breed with a Graced?

The last issue was Naomi's greatest concern. There were rumors – old, old rumors – that vampires and weres had once been able to have children with her species, and that's why the Graced had wiped everyone's memories of their existence. They'd been sick of being stolen, raped and tortured, used to swell the vampire and were ranks while decimating their own.

There were so many questions, and as a Gray rather than a Green, Naomi had no real way to get answers. It wasn't like she could simply introduce herself to the girl and have a little chat.

Well, she *could*, but she didn't see that working out too well.

Movement caught her attention, and Naomi saw Monique being counter-balanced by her companion while lowering a bow.

Lowering a bow? Naomi whipped her head back to Subject 2013.

Aria Ash staggered, an arrow in the center of her chest.

No.

Naomi threw her hand out, but it was too late. The girl was as good as dead. A wooden arrow to the heart? She was part vampire, after all.

The hybrid let out a startled shout and dropped to her knees on the gravel-covered ground. Other cries then sounded, and footsteps pounded toward the courtyard. A man appeared, his speed of movement something to wonder at.

It was the were from the forest. He was shirtless, and his hair was tied back in a ponytail, but he moved like the predator he was.

"ARIA!"

Vampire guards were arriving now, too, swords out and at the ready. Crouching next to the girl, the were cradled her in his arms, but she struggled against the hold. Pushing herself to her feet, Subject 2013 wobbled a little and then straightened. She was alive.

How could she be?

The hybrid snapped the arrow in half, pulling the point from her back, then turned to the wall.

"Run!" Monique's yell shattered the air.

She and her companion turned to leap off the wall, but the hybrid was already running, her arm snapping out with incredible speed and throwing the broken arrow like a spear. A soft thud, and Naomi watched in horror as Monique's companion dropped from the ledge, impaled. The hybrid kept running though, straight for the wall, the werewolf close at her heels.

The Hunter was dead before he hit the ground.

Monique had launched herself off the wall the moment Subject 2013 had broken the arrow. She landed with a thud on the cobbles outside the estate, and took off at a sprint down the darkened street, toward the busiest part of town. No doubt she hoped to mask her scent in the crowds.

Subject 2013 paused at the top of the wall, looking toward where Monique had been. Her eyes then travelled over Naomi's hiding place, but she gave her head a shake, and then jumped from the wall to land at the dead man's feet.

The hybrid's voice travelled up to Naomi. "He wasn't alone."

"It smells like someone is still here, but I can't see any one."

Naomi blanched. She thought her shield also muddied her scent, but obviously it needed a bit more tweaking when it came to fooling were senses. They were stronger than she'd assumed.

The were placed a careful hand on Subject 2013's shoulder. "Can you track them?"

The hybrid was rubbing her chest. "Probably, but I am not really up to running around town. That bloody arrow pierced my heart."

"*What?*"

"Aria!" The Duke of Ashes himself had arrived.

Naomi shrank back against the stone of the wall. She'd seen the vampire before during her surveillance of his daughter, but never this close. He was intimidating, to say the least. Her pulse raced in trepidation just from looking at him. Tall and muscular, with ash-blond hair, he was enough to make most women throw caution to the wind and climb into bed with him. Or just take him where he stood.

Naomi.

Funny how her conscience suddenly sounded like her sister, Marcia. Her elder sibling would have been traumatized by that thought.

But her thoughts didn't matter, because Parker Ash's eyes were a deep purple, which meant he was a vampire through and through, and he was confident in his power and position in society. And he was just as ruthless.

He reached a hand out, as if to touch his daughter, then pulled it back. "There's blood on you, what happened?"

"Someone shot her in the heart with a bloody arrow."

The full-blooded vampire looked up, eyes tracing over the stone wall, lingering on Naomi's location. He wouldn't be able to see her, she knew that, but she couldn't stop the involuntary swallow when his gaze locked on her, then darted away.

The duke turned his attention back to his daughter. "Why did he attack you?"

"It's not like I had time to stop and take tea with him, Father. He's dead."

Interestingly, Subject 2013 was beginning to look a little queasy, as if the body at her feet bothered her.

"There was a second person, but they got away," the were said, nodding in the direction of the city. "I will go after them, I think I have a scent."

"Do it."

The were gave Subject 2013 a long look, and then sprinted off into the streets, following Monique. Naomi wondered if he'd be able to catch the Green-eyed woman.

Then the duke was shepherding his daughter into the estate. "Come back inside, let's get the wound checked out."

"It's already healing," she said, but she went with the vampire anyway.

As they passed under the arch in the wall near Naomi, she heard the duke ask, "What was it made from?"

"Wood."

So, a wooden implement to the heart wasn't enough to kill the hybrid?

Fascinating.

CHAPTER EIGHTEEN

The other attacker had vanished. Once they'd reached the busy streets, there were so many scents all tangled together that Sebastian couldn't pick out the archer's. What did strike him as strange were the glazed expressions some of the people wore as they stood about in the street, like all the nearby humans had been summoned out to mingle with each other, just to confuse the trail.

Growling low in frustration, he headed back to the Grumpy Bear. It was early morning, and the vampires were still out and about on their social whirl. Not wanting to bump into any of them – or even just get close enough to be asked why he smelled of blood – he headed down the back streets. They were narrow and stank of urine, but at least that was better than having to deal with aristos.

He fucking had to find the person who'd hurt Aria, but there was no point in pursuing anything further tonight. The assailant was long gone. Someone had been following her, though, and he'd bet his eyeteeth the attacker would try again. They'd be back to finish the job.

Over my dead body.

It might come to that, he realized.

Aria had been shot in the *chest* by a wooden arrow *and survived.* Somehow, her weird bloodline had saved her. Yet when he'd heard her cry out, the adrenalin... He'd been just outside the estate, lingering nearby like a lovesick fool, rather than returning to the inn. At the sound of her pain, he'd bolted to her as fast as he could, in time to see her drop to her knees.

He'd thought she was dying.

Agony had roared through him. He'd just found her, only to lose her so soon? How had he managed to fail her twice? Allowed her get hurt so soon after she'd changed everything for him?

But she'd shrugged him away, stood up and thrown that arrow like a fucking javelin. It had been astounding. Especially when she'd hit one of the two humans who'd been squatting on the stone wall like deranged pigeons.

Even now, he wanted to rush back to her side, but that probably wouldn't go down all that well. She'd proven to him time and again she was strong, that she didn't need his help. It didn't stop him from wanting to give it to her, though. Plus, Ash had been with her, so maybe it wasn't the best time for him to visit. He didn't want her father knowing about what was developing between them.

Sebastian stopped outside the inn, opened the door and ducked inside. Without even stopping to give the taproom a quick once-over, he made straight for the stairs.

"Sebastian!"

He turned toward the sound of his name; a woman was waving at him from one of the leather chairs near the fire.

Sebastian's mouth dried up. Her hair was snow white, and her skin just as pale; he couldn't quite see the color of her eyes from where he stood, but he had a feeling they'd be pink. Her pale hair was woven with string, beads and bones, and some strands had been dyed blue and green. She wore a strange tunic over tan-colored pants, and looked about as comfortable as you could get.

It was the woman he'd spotted the other day, and as he drew closer, it was plain she was an albino. He was halfway to the chair opposite her before he'd even consciously acknowledged they were going to chat.

He stopped, noting absently that the fire was burning pathetically low. She was pretty with her pink eyes, this woman. Not beautiful like Aria, but definitely striking. How had she managed to survive to adulthood?

"Sebastian, nice to see you."

"Have we met?" Maybe she'd heard Milly the innkeeper using his name?

"I guess not." She flicked away a few strands of hair that had spilled over her shoulder. "Sorry, this kind of thing tends to happen a lot."

"It does?" He sat down, the leather chair squeaking a little as it molded to his body.

"You ever wonder why all those albino children you've been trying to save are hunted down like rabid animals?"

How had she known about his 'hobby'?

Who *was* this woman?

"Of course." He had wondered about that *a lot*. Why kill defenseless babies? What could possibly be gained? Sure, some of the kids were, well, odd. Not quite living in the present, but saying that they could sometimes see the future. While he'd spent half of his life saving all the kids he could, he hadn't really stuck around to see how they'd developed in their new homes, but he kept track of their progress. It was crushing to learn that about half of them were dead by the time they turned twenty. Most of their lives were taken by their own hand.

"Have you ever noticed how few humans have eye colors other than Brown?"

He frowned. What had this to do with albino children? "Not really." He didn't spend much time with humans.

"Well, if you had looked around, you'd see that it's fairly rare for humans to have Blue, Green or Gray eyes."

The way she said the colors... like she was putting extra emphasis on the words. Like names. "So?"

"What is Pink then, if not another color?"

"I don't get it."

She sighed, and pinched the bridge of her nose. "Argh. Okay. You know the origin story of vampires and weres, at least?"

"That we evolved out of humans?" People didn't

really talk about how the species had appeared – they just had.

She shook her head. "Incorrect."

"What?"

"Vampires and weres were *made by humans. That's* a bit different: being created, versus evolving."

He laughed. "That's ridiculous. How could they *make* us?"

"They don't have the technology anymore, but they once had." Her eyes had developed a faraway look, like she was seeing through him into another time. "It was before my day."

How old *was* she?

"Look, I have other things to do…" He made to stand up.

"Like saving that half-breed girlfriend of yours?"

He froze. "What did you say?"

"You heard me. I know all about Aria Ash and her issues. I'm willing to help you both, but first, you have to hear me out."

"I don't have to do anything."

"Fine. Leave. But when everything goes wrong, remember that I could have helped you."

He sat back down. "When what goes wrong?"

"Not yet." She tapped her leg. "What I am about to tell you is considered to be very secret. If you reveal it to people, they will track you down and kill you."

"Who will?"

"Hunters."

He was getting a headache. "Who are the hunters?"

"People with colored eyes."

"And why do people with colored eyes want to kill me?"

"They don't right now, but they will if you blab."

"I'm confused." Man, more than confused. "Okay, how about we start at the beginning?"

She rolled her eyes. "I was *trying* to do that."

"With humans with colored eyes?"

"*Yes*. You're finally starting to get it."

He really wasn't.

"Let's try again."

Her sigh was long-suffering. "So, humans made vampires and weres, but they also made another sub-species of human. They are called the Graced, and they are humans with eye colors other than Brown. You following?"

"Vaguely."

"So, early on, all four races were relatively close, genetically speaking. It meant they could interbreed; well, except for normal humans. But after years of war and other things I don't have time to go into, they began to separate out. Vampires could only breed with vampires, and weres with weres. But, back in the beginning, it was *possible* for them to have kids with each other, and with the Graced – the people with colored eyes."

"So anyone with colored eyes is Graced?"

"Yes, except for vampires or weres."

"You have colored eyes."

"Exactly."

"But you smell a bit like wolf."

"My parents were weres."

Sebastian's headache was getting worse by the minute. "So you are a were but also Graced."

"Yes, I am one of the few who are both."

"But what does being Graced *mean*?"

"People with colored eyes have special abilities. I'm sure that you've noticed that the kids you've saved have been…different."

He didn't really know what to say to that, so he just nodded.

"People with Blue eyes can read emotions; Gray eyed people can move things with their will, and Greens can read other people's minds. People with Pink eyes – I do prefer to call them Red, but today is honesty day – can see the future."

His heartbeat paused for a moment, then kicked back in, drumming loudly. So she thought she could see the future. And the crazy thing? He kind of believed her. Some of the kids he'd saved had told him the same thing.

"Is that why they kill themselves?"

Her expression grew sad. "I can't see the future of other Pinks, so I can't say with certainty, but yes, I'd guess that would be the case. Seeing the future, all the possible outcomes, choices, decisions, and how they impact, yes, it would be enough to make someone want it to…stop. Some Pinks only ever see glimpses, some see it all. It can be overwhelming, and some might do whatever it takes to end the visions."

Sebastian swallowed. He couldn't imagine what a life like that would be like. Had he done the right thing, in saving those children? "You said you know about Aria?"

"She was born to a fourth-generation vampire, and a fourth-generation were. They beat the odds. I didn't know about her until her last brother died, though. I couldn't see her future with him nearby."

Xave had been albino. *So Xave is dead.*

No wonder Aria was furious with the world.

He sat forward. "What's going to happen to her?"

"Well, I can't say right now. There's too many choices to be made."

"But you told me—"

"That I'd help." She stood. "Just not right now."

She turned to leave the taproom.

"Wait, what's your name?" Sebastian asked.

"Oh, I forgot. It's Ralia Lovett. You can call me Lia."

"Lia." Lovett, he *knew* that surname for some reason.

"And don't forget about what I said. You talk to anyone – even Aria – about this, and they'll find out and hunt you down."

Then she was gone, leaving him with more questions than answers.

CHAPTER NINETEEN

"She fucking killed him!" Monique slammed down her tankard of ale on the scarred table of the inn.

The tavern was about as shady as they came in Skarva; drugs, food, alcohol and flesh for sale. The only thing it was missing was blood, and that was only because it catered to human clientele, rather than vampire. Naomi had hidden herself in the next booth over, the thick cloud of tobacco smoke assisting her sight-shield in hiding her identity. Her sight-shield was one of the more difficult telekinetic feats she'd mastered, and one that wasn't widely known about. The fact she'd done it as a child…well, extra points for her.

"But you said the shot was true?" Monique's companion asked. Naomi couldn't see the other woman's face due to the angle and hovering smoke, but her shoulders were slumped with age.

"Yes," Monique snapped. "Vince made sure it was."

So, he must have been another Gray. *Obviously not*

a talented one; to get struck through the heart. Even if the arrow had sped through the air like lightning, Naomi would have been able to deflect it with her ability.

"And she didn't die?" The older woman's voice rose, in disbelief or anger, Naomi couldn't tell. "From a wooden arrow to the heart?"

Monique shook her head. "No, she pulled it out of her own bloody chest."

The older woman leaned back. "Then it's the right girl."

"But Vince is *dead*." The redhaired Hunter's words were low, angry.

"There are casualties in any war. You know that."

The speaker was stone cold, but her logic was sound. Most people had no clue there was a war being fought daily – one so dangerous that if you participated, you had to come to terms with the fact you could die at any moment.

Vampires and weres did not take kindly to interference in their rule. And humans, well, they were just as capable of the atrocities their immortal overlords were renowned for.

"Too many good people have died, if you ask me," Monique muttered.

"Not this *again*."

Stubborn silence.

Interesting. Naomi wouldn't have pinned Monique as the type to have a conscience. Not when she forced her way into people's minds and stole their thoughts on a daily basis.

"That whole pack was slaughtered," Monique said quietly, voice intense as she leaned toward the other woman. "Is that what you want to happen to us?"

"Not all of them."

"Fine. Most of the pack was slaughtered."

"I had no idea that the she-wolf would be so protective of her mutant offspring."

"Most mothers would do anything to protect their children."

"So I've heard." Her voice was dry.

Naomi hoped that Monique's companion wasn't the older woman from the forest; that lady had looked awfully similar to the younger Green-eyed Hunter. If she was, their mother-daughter relationship was really screwed up. Even Naomi could pick out the undertones.

"Why not just program that wolf she's spending time with to kill her and be done with it?" the redhead demanded.

That was more like the Monique Naomi knew: busy trying to make other people do her dirty work.

"He has a natural shield, which you'd know if you'd been spying properly. And he's not alone in that cursed pack. Three other members of the pack were immune as well. It's phenomenal. It's rare to find that level of resistance to a Green of our abilities. I had to wait until he had left before I could coerce the other pack members into hunting down the children. Even then, the mother killed most of them. The alpha finished them off afterwards. The fact that he's back in town is a bad sign."

So Subject 2013 had known the were before? Maybe that explained the nightly forest visits. It had nothing to do with romance at all, and everything to do with a shared history.

"You could have just said no," Monique said.

The other woman ignored the verbal jab. "We want to attack her when she's alone."

Monique let out a short burst of laughter. It did not sound the slightest bit happy. "She's never alone."

"That's ridiculous."

"No, it's true. If she's not surrounded by servants, her father – who also has a mental shield – is there, or that wolf is nearby. And then there's bloody Naomi Castle."

Awww, she didn't know they cared about her that much.

"One of the Castles is *here*?"

"She's been following the abomination as well."

"That isn't good news. Why didn't you tell me before?"

"I gave her a bit of an incentive to stay away, but if she's anything like that sister of hers, she won't stay gone for long."

Naomi hadn't stayed away at all. After the migraine had worn off, she'd been back out on the streets, following her quarry. Even if she'd had to mop up a nose bleed or three during that time.

"I'll set one of the others on the job."

"What job?"

"Making sure Castle isn't in our way."

Naomi didn't like the sound of that one bit.

CHAPTER TWENTY

She'd *killed* someone.

I'm not a murderer.

The facts didn't lie though, did they? Ari had seen that body sprawled on the ground, the back of his skull shattered on the cobblestones, the arrow protruding obscenely from his chest. *She'd* done that.

For the millionth time, she fought the urge to vomit, and burrowed into the bedspread and mattress even further. She'd returned to the estate, showered, and then crept into her bed after the city coroner had trundled away with the body. Death was so final, so absolute. And she'd cut short a *human's* life – when their time was so brief to begin with.

Guilt gnawed at her.

They shot you with an arrow.

Yet it didn't kill her, had barely even slowed her down, although they couldn't have known that would happen.

They deserved it.

No one deserved to die.

A voice growled at her, *If they hurt us or those we care about, then they do.*

He wolf was *speaking* to her.

Why won't you come out? she thought back.

Can't. A small whine in the back of her mind. *Hurts.*

Well, that was it. She was crazy. She was talking to her inner wolf like it was another person. Ari had always thought it as more like a sister than a part of her, and she'd somehow split it into its own entity. Great. She really *had* broken herself.

The shutter on her window banged and the scent of caramel and figs hit her. She didn't even emerge from her blanket cocoon. "Did you find the other shooter?"

The mattress dipped as Sebastian sat on the edge of the bed. His voice was low, rough. "No."

Part of her was happy about that, really happy. There'd be one less death tonight. Sebastian would have killed the archer, no doubt about it. Ari had finally come to understand that he wouldn't hurt her, but would harm anyone who dared try. Too bad he hadn't been there for her when she really needed it.

He peered over the top of her blankets, his gaze bright. "I'm sorry."

"It's okay."

"No, it's not."

He lay back on the bed, hands tucked behind his head. She rolled over, drawn toward him. He had a new shirt on, and a jacket, although his pants were still the same, and his hair was out, spreading over her pillow like a cloud of raven silk. Her fingers itched to touch it.

She clenched her fingers into a fist. "I don't know why they're after me."

"You don't?" He looked at her exposed yellow eye; she hadn't bothered putting the patch back on after her shower.

"No one knows, I've been really careful." She had, plus she'd blackmailed anyone who had ever claimed she wasn't what she seemed.

Sebastian sat up and then took hold of her, blankets and all, before lying back and tucking her against him. She tensed, waiting for something else to happen, but nothing did. Eventually, she relaxed against him. It felt...nice. She'd never really cuddled before.

In the past, all of her romantic relationships had died quick deaths. Inevitability, her partners wanted access to parts of her that were *hers,* and she couldn't share the secrets of herself, not without putting other people at risk. When there was no trust, there couldn't be anything more, and she wasn't about to hurt someone just so she could get laid. She'd stopped bothering, after a while.

"I can't think of another reason why someone would want to hurt you."

With her ear pressed to the smooth planes of his chest, she felt more than heard his words. She looked up at him, her mouth quirking in a half-smile. "You can't?"

"I'm not going to answer that."

A soft laugh escaped her. "If we were to ignore my wonderful personality for a few moments, there's the fact that the Duke of Ashes is my father. He has a few enemies. It wouldn't surprise me if one of them went after me to get at him."

It was more likely than someone wanting to kill her because of her mismatched eyes, anyway.

Sebastian gently stroked her hair. "What luck you've had."

That was one way to put it.

His hand swept down her back, leaving a trail of fire in its wake. Her skin tingled, the remembered taste of his blood making her crave him *in* her. How could he evoke such responses from her? He made her feel so *alive*. Ari propped herself up on her elbow and then leaned down, her mouth an inch from his. "Want to try and change my luck around?"

"You need to rest." He frowned. "You got shot in the chest."

She sat up, lifted an eyebrow. "I can show you the scar."

"You have a scar?" The idea had him sitting upright, too.

"You'll have to wait and see." She dropped the bedding around her, and then pulled her shirt off. His eyes went wide, locking on her breasts. Her nipples tightened at the attention.

He shoved a pillow over his lap. "You need to put your shirt back on."

She fought a smile. "Weren't you going to check the scar?" She ran a fingertip between her breasts.

His eyes clamped shut. "Shirt."

Oh, he was trying to be noble. That wasn't going to do at all. Ari leaned forward and nipped his lip.

"What?"

"I feel *fine*."

"You were shot."

"Want to kiss it better?"

A low groan and then he was moving away from her – to the edge of the bed. She pounced after him, pinning him down and straddling him. He struggled, but that just thrust his cock against her sex, creating delicious friction. He cursed and lay still. "How is it you're so tiny, but you're also so strong?"

"Awesomeness."

He huffed.

She pressed her body down and moved against his erection. They both groaned.

"Aria, this is a bad idea."

"Why?"

"You're injured."

"I'm healed."

"You hate me."

"Haven't your heard? Hate sex can be good."

His gaze narrowed to menacing slits.

"Fine. I don't hate you – as much – anymore."

"You blame me for your brother's death."

"That will take me a little longer to get over. But I believe that you didn't order it." That understanding had come over the past week, slowly and begrudgingly.

"You—"

She'd had enough. Why did he always get chatty at the worst times? She pressed her upper body against his torso, and then licked her way up his neck. Mmm. Salted caramel. He breathed out slowly, hardening even more against her. Despite wanting to do the right thing, his body still desired her. And she desired him.

She ran a feather-light kiss over his lips, then bit down hard on his chin.

"Ow!"

"Kiss me."

"You're too bossy."

"You like it."

He moved, twisting her underneath him, his mouth fusing to hers, igniting a fire in her blood. Warmth pooled between her legs, and she reached down, gripping his erection firmly, stroking it. "I want this inside me."

"Ari—"

She increased the tempo.

"If you don't stop, I'll come now."

"Take off your pants."

He did, then removed hers, his claws slashing out and shredding them. She loved it. Soon after, his tongue swirled its way up her inner thigh, driving her mad. "I have to taste you."

"Not now." She couldn't wait, had to have him in her *now*. Flipping them both over, she straddled him again, and then sank down on his length in one hard thrust. He moaned her name as she gasped. He stretched her, filled her up to bursting, and it was wonderful. Shutting her eyes, she savored the sensation.

"Aria?"

"Mmmm?"

"Are you okay?"

"Yes." In fact, she was better than okay. She felt…peaceful. Like this joining was meant to be, that he was a part of her that should never have been separated.

"Good." And then he turned her on her back again and began to thrust. Pleasure exploded through her and she clutched at him. This was perfect. No matter what the world threw at her, this was perfect.

CHAPTER TWENTY-ONE

"Blood and pain and death."

Xave's words echoed in her mind as Ari walked through the forest, Sebastian – in human form – by her side. The scent of rain lingered in the air, along with the astringency of various plants, the musky tang of small mammals, and the ever-present mouth-watering aroma of Sebastian.

The call of night birds, along with the skittering and crunching of various animals made the forest come alive after dark. The towering oak trees meant little moonlight reached them in the depths of the foliage, but that was fine with her. Wolves didn't rely on their vision when it came to hunting, and hers was perfect anyway.

Blood and pain and death.

There had already *been* blood and pain and death, but it hadn't broken her like Xave had said it would. Guilt still gnawed at her over the human's death – she hadn't wanted to become a killer, to take someone like she'd had people taken from her. As her father said, however, it was survival of the fittest.

To be weak was to be dead.

And she didn't want to die.

"You said your wolf hurts?"

Snapping her attention back to the present, she looked at the solid tree behind Sebastian's right shoulder. It had strange, wormlike patterns over its trunk, patterns she couldn't place... "She does."

"Hrm."

She didn't like the subtext of the syllable, but she wasn't about to get into a debate with him about 'merging with her wolf'. If she knew how, she would have done it already.

Ari was walking along the deer track when the silence finally registered. Everything had gone quiet. Peering over her shoulder, she held up a finger to her lips, but Sebastian already had his head tipped back, nose in the air. Inhaling deeply, she searched for scents that shouldn't be here.

There. Sweat, metal, horses...and humans.

They were surrounded.

She turned in a slow circle, the better to pinpoint people in the trees, but there was no one. Strange. If she could smell them, then she should be able to see them. Something wasn't right.

"How many do you detect?" Her voice was low, so the humans wouldn't be able to hear it.

"Roughly four."

Four. That should be easy. If she could find them.

He sidled up next to her, growling low in his throat. "One smells familiar."

"My shooter?"

He nodded.

Great. They hadn't given up like she'd hoped. The human's death must have incited them. Why couldn't they see that if they'd left her alone, he'd still be alive? Why come for revenge?

A shadow flickered in the distance, and Ari spun toward it. She was moving fast when a howl of pain stopped her. Sebastian was flying through the air, as if he'd been thrown. His back slammed into the tree she'd been staring at earlier with a meaty thud.

"Sebastian!" Her eyes scanned madly for an attacker, but she couldn't spot anyone.

His yellow gaze turned wild as he struggled, but he couldn't seem to peel himself away from the tree. It *looked* like he was being held down, but there was no one there.

"I'm stuck!"

What is happening?

She sprinted to him as the sickening sound of breaking bone shattered the air. Sebastian let out an agonized growl, and sweat beaded across his forehead. Ari skidded to a stop. His arm was bent at an unnatural angle. *How?*

Where *was* the bloody attacker?

A high-pitched whistle reached her ears, followed by a series of soft thuds. Four darts had embedded in Sebastian's chest. Quickly, she plucked them out, murmuring useless words of comfort. Each dart had a glass chamber that held fluid – chambers that were now empty except for traces of a gleaming metallic liquid. She ripped Sebastian's shirt open, exposing puncture wounds that were already turning black.

Silver poisoning.

She stared at his face, his bronze skin ashen. "How do I help? What do I do?"

"Nothing."

That hadn't been Sebastian.

Whirling around, Ari clenched a dart in her hand so hard the glass broke, silver droplets dripping onto the leaf-covered ground like blood. A figure emerged from the shadows, stepping cautiously into the small area: it was an older human, with wide green eyes and faded red hair. Most importantly, she was covered in weapons.

"Who are you?" Ari opened her hand and let the debris fall away.

"My identity is unimportant."

"I would argue against that."

"Co-operate and the were lives. Be difficult, and he will die in front of you. It's that simple."

"Why do I get the feeling he's dead anyway?"

A smirk. That was it.

How dare this woman try and take what's ours? her wolf growled.

"We only seek your death. We don't care about the were."

"How charitable of you."

Suddenly phantom fingers were tugging at Ari's eye-patch. She grabbed onto the strap, and craned her neck, but there was no one nearby. How were these people doing it? The patch broke, falling away from her head, and she shut her eye in reflex. She couldn't let these people see the secret she'd spent years hiding.

"Open your eye."

"No."

"Open it."

"No."

Her head exploded in agony, like she'd been hit in the skull by a twenty-ton rock. Her vision blacked out, and her knees gave way. Every beat of her heart exacerbated the pain, until all she could sense was suffering so intense she'd become blind to the world.

"Aria!"

Sebastian was calling her, but she couldn't draw breath to respond. The pain escalated, driving through her, and then every bone in her body was breaking, shattering, reforming into something new. Her face melted under the pressure and a new form took place.

Her wolf was free.

"I always wondered if you could shift," the woman said. "Turns out you just needed a little…motivation."

Her vision slowly began to come back, hazy and fuzzy and then crystallizing sharp and clear. The woman was closer now, only a few body lengths away. She smelt of death; sweet, pungent rot.

We hurt her now? her wolf asked.

Even though her wolf was now in charge of her body, the animalistic side of her still sought Ari's approval.

Soon.

Ari growled at the woman, a warning. *Come no closer.*

The human just smiled. "You don't know how many years I've been waiting to finish this."

Ari tilted her head to the side. She'd never seen this woman before in her life.

"Come now, surely you remember that night when the pack turned on you?"

Ari froze.

"Well, they needed a little motivation to get started. I provided it. Except you and that other brother of yours escaped."

This woman had been responsible for Mama's and Nick's deaths? How? She was a human. Weres did *not* obey human commands.

"Ridiculous!" Sebastian's voice thundered through the small area.

"Really? You know how strong a bond is with an alpha." Her voice was taunting. "It isn't an easy thing to break."

"Then how did you manage to do it?" he demanded.

"Come now, you were alpha. You knew this freak and her brother. You know that some humans are different."

"You're saying *you* convinced the pack to turn on us with your *mind*?"

CHAPTER TWENTY-TWO

Parker Ash wasn't prone to emotional outbursts, but he was slowly approaching the point where he was about to snap. Someone was stalking him. Or Aria. He didn't know which, but he didn't like it one bit.

No one came after his family.

No one.

The only trouble with the situation? He didn't know who the stalker *was*. He thought he'd spotted them once or twice, but the image would blur before he could get a lock on their face. A flash of strawberry blonde hair and a glimpse of wide, gray eyes; that was all he'd processed. Tonight, he'd sensed them again – on the wall, some distance from where Aria had been shot – and had tried to pinpoint them, only to have them vanish. How they kept escaping his senses, he had no idea.

It didn't matter; he was still going to hunt them down. And not because something about that gray gaze haunted him.

"Your Grace."

He glanced up from his desk, and his heart shuddered. An albino woman stood before him, just inside the door, her skin glowing under the gas lighting, her hair decorated with bones and shells, and dyed strands. He closed and reopened his eyes to see if she'd vanish, but she was still there.

"How did you get in here?"

She gave a little shrug. "Through the door."

The door. Right.

He sat back in his chair unable to avoid seeing something of his son in this woman. Xavier would have been sixty this year, as would Nick, the child he'd never even met. Rage still clouded his vision when he thought of that poor boy, dying in a fit of were madness, knowing his end was coming. The duke was well aware that Nick had been like Xavier – that they'd been special. The future had been something that was all too visible for Xavier, and he'd seen it with such depth and clarity that it drove him insane.

That's why he had listened to his son's pleas when Aria had refused to. She was tough like steel, but also brittle. She would do anything to keep her loved ones close, even if it was better to set them free. It had broken him that day, when he'd had to kill his boy, but Xavier had craved death like a drunk craved alcohol. Parker had learned a long time ago that holding on to someone for yourself didn't help the person you were trying to save.

They had to *want* to be saved.

He nodded at the stranger. "Why have you decided to pay me a visit?"

The woman strode forward and seated herself opposite him at the metal desk. She flicked out her tunic-shirt then crossed her legs, and the faint scent of wolf reached him.

So she'd been born to were parents, and she was alive. He ground his teeth, battling his envy.

"It isn't so much a decision as a need." She gave a half smile as her fingers traced patterns on her knee. He was tempted to lean forward to see what shapes she'd drawn. He'd learned from Xavier that nothing was irrelevant when it came to albinos. His son had predicted his own death long before it had ever occurred and had extracted a promise Parker had never believed he'd have to fulfill.

"My name is Parker Ash," he said. "And you are?"

"I know who you are, Duke of Ashes. I am Ralia Lovett."

Lovett. Yes, he knew that name, but he'd never heard of an albino were associated with it. Clay Lovett was an old werewolf, third generation, and he'd been travelling around the continent for longer than Parker had been alive. Was she a daughter? Sister? Mother? With people so long-lived, the family relationships got complicated.

"And why do you feel the need to visit?"

"I may have muddled my timing up a little."

"Your timing?" His gut sank.

"Yes, I thought that Aria would have a little longer with Sebastian before...well, before. But I was out. It happens. It's hard to see exactly *when* things will occur, there's just so many factors..." Her pink gaze turned inward.

The expression was like a punch in the face. How often had his son worn that exact same look?

"So when do you think it will happen?" he asked. Not that he had any idea what 'it' was, but then, if it involved the alpha and his daughter, it was bound to be volatile.

"About now."

He wasn't about to lose another child. Especially not Aria. It's why he'd contacted the bloody were in the first place; her shifting was a problem, and that meant it was a weakness. He needed his daughter to be as strong as possible.

He stood. "What do I need to do?"

She eyed him for a few moments and he fought the urge to fidget. Parker was *not* prone to fidgeting.

At last, she said, "Follow me."

CHAPTER TWENTY-THREE

Pain slashed through Sebastian; his broken arm hadn't been set properly, and was healing incorrectly. If he got out of here alive, he was going to have to re-break it and enjoy having his arm mend itself all over again. At least that would only take a few hours.

The only part he was iffy about was surviving, thanks to the slow burn of acid rolling through his veins. They'd shot him with *four darts* of liquid silver. His organs were fighting it, but the poison was spreading through his whole body.

The human woman was glaring at him; something dangerous flashing in her Green eyes. Lia's warning blared throughout his mind: if they found out he knew about the Graced, they'd come for him. But she would have no idea he knew anything, not unless she could read his mind.

Could she?

The woman didn't react to that thought, so he had to wonder... but Lia had said Green was for telepathy. Blue was for emotions and stuff, and

Gray…well, that explained why he was plastered to a tree trunk. There had to be someone with Gray eyes hiding in the forest.

Was everyone susceptible to these abilities, or were there people with natural protections? He wished he'd paid more attention to Lia, because he hadn't realized what she'd said was a warning, dressed up as history.

Were they after Aria because she'd known there was something different about her brother? No wait, this woman had said she'd had something to do with the pack's deaths all those years ago. Sebastian's eyes drifted to his lover – she was a petite wolf, all lean lines and elegant angles. Her amber fur was draped in torn clothing, which had survived her shift. He mouthed, "It'll be okay."

Another woman stepped out of the trees, a younger version of his tormentor. Sebastian struggled against the invisible force that held him.

The newcomer stayed close to a large oak. "Just finish this and let's go."

"Fine," the older woman said. "I just thought I'd give the abomination some closure." She turned and stared at Aria.

A scream tore through the clearing and the small wolf writhed in pain. Fur melted away, bones broke, and then Aria was lying on the forest floor, naked.

She was *forcing* Aria to shift.

Aria lay panting as the older woman knelt next to her, a dagger held high in one hand. One side gleamed like metal, the other was dull, like wood. Her arm swung downward—

"*No!*" Sebastian bellowed as he fought, but he was still stuck. He could only watch as that human killed Aria. *Not again. Not* her.

"Stop!"

The knife-wielder was lifted and thrown through the air like a ragdoll. She hit a nearby tree with a crunching of bones and fell limp to the ground. Sebastian's desperate gaze swung back to Aria; she lay immobile, the weapon's hilt protruding from her chest.

"*Aria!*"

He struggled anew, fighting to get to her. She'd survived the wooden arrow, but both silver and wood at the same time…

A third woman was emerging from the trees now, a strawberry blonde. Sebastian had never seen her before, but from her large Gray eyes he guessed she must have been the one who'd thrown Aria's attacker across the forest.

"You!" The younger woman glared at the new arrival. "I told you to stay away, Castle!"

The blonde – Castle – gave a strange smile. "But then I'd miss all the fun."

"I told you what would happen." The redhead advanced on her. *At least she's moving away from Aria.*

"And I warned you not to mess with me."

Great, Sebastian thought. *A pissing contest.*

Two men burst into sight, their expressions panicked. The hold on Sebastian wavered, and he shoved against the tree, but with no luck. He was still pinned. Maybe this Castle would help him.

Castle's expression grew serious. "Three against

one? That's hardly fair."

"You've got it coming."

"Actually, I meant for you."

The two men flew into the air, tossed away like toys. One slowed quicker than the other, flipping in a somersault before landing. The earth exploded around Castle, soil launching high, and a tree trunk was torn free with a rip. It floated in the air and then zoomed toward the two men, hitting one hard across the head.

The vice around Sebastian vanished. He ran toward Aria, ducking low to avoid being hit by the bits of forest these people were throwing at each other.

Who used a tree as a weapon, anyway?

He skidded to a stop next to Aria. She was pale, but breathing, sweat dotting her forehead. Sebastian stared at the knife hilt. Pull it out, or leave it in? *Out*, he decided. With a sharp tug, he ripped the blade free – her body was already healing around it. Aria gasped, her eyes snapping open, and she inhaled in a hard, raspy draw. She jackknifed upright, hands pressed to her chest.

"Sebastian?"

He leaned down to grab her as a scream of rage rent the night. Castle was hovering in the air, her hair blown back by a wind he couldn't feel. Blood leaked from her nose, and her eyes blazed. Her teeth were bared, smeared with crimson.

"Get the fuck out of my head, Monique!"

"Just go and you'll live!" the redhead spat.

Both men were back on their feet now, one

staggering, and they threw out their hands, just as Monique created a fist. Castle groaned, and then she was flying back through the air. Sebastian didn't see where she landed, but there was a loud crack.

Fuck. That was it then; their only help was probably dead. Quickly, he gathered Aria into his arms.

Time to get out of here.

Except Monique was there, standing in his path.

"Not so fast."

CHAPTER TWENTY-FOUR

Naomi's head *hurt*.

Just her head, though. The rest of her body –
nothing.

Panic clawed its way up through her throat as the
dizziness subsided. Her hands and feet, there was no
sensation there at all. Shouts echoed in her ears,
though, which meant the battle was still being waged
and that her hearing worked. Thank goodness for
small mercies.

She willed her muscles to move her hand; nothing
happened. She just lay on the leaf litter like a broken
doll. Wetness dripped into her eyes and without a
hand to wipe it away, she used her powers.

I have a broken neck.

Or something horribly like it. She'd been flung out
of the fight by the two Gray males. Normally, they
wouldn't have been an issue for Naomi, but they'd
managed it because Monique had clawed her way
inside her mind first. If not for that, she'd still be in
the fight. Blood, she probably would have *ended* it by

now.

Using her telekinesis, she lifted her limp body off the ground, steadying it and straightening her spine until she looked like she was standing. Then she glided through the air toward the yells and obscenities. On the edge of the fight, she could see the alpha, injured and struggling to pick up Subject 2013. Naomi had been late to this particular party, so she hadn't seen the first strikes, but she could guess: darts filled with liquid silver, no doubt. It was a new favorite of the Graced.

Her eyes narrowed on the two Gray men. One was helping Monique's relative, the other was staring at the were. The alpha rose, levitating off the ground, but it was slow. The Gray must be weakening. It happened. When it came to their powers, not all Graced were equal.

Naomi spared one last glance at the older woman. She hoped she hadn't hurt her irrevocably when she'd thrown her, but then, that woman was responsible for more deaths than most vampires. Maybe her demise would be a blessing.

You are not to judge.

That was exactly why she'd chosen to go against her family's path: they acted as judge, jury and executioner for those that didn't comply with their laws. Naomi hadn't wanted blood on her hands – still didn't – but sometimes you had to make the hard choices, and there were two innocent lives at stake.

Well, relatively innocent. Naomi was convinced Subject 2013 was a blackmailer, and who knew what the were had done? But in all the time she'd been following the hybrid, Naomi had never seen the girl kill or hurt anyone aside from the man who had attacked her with Monique. That spoke volumes.

Ignoring the pain ricocheting through her skull, she focused on the Gray closet to her. Methodically, she snapped his forearms and shin bones – clean breaks, so that they'd heal nicely, but breaks nonetheless. And perhaps she'd gone for *both* arms and legs because of her neck. Payback was a bitch.

The man screamed, high-pitched and ear-splitting. Before he finished, she'd broken the other Gray's arms and legs, too. Snap, snap, snap, snap. Sure, she could have killed both of them; crushed them until they'd resembled nothing more than pulverized meat, but pain was enough. When it came to telekinesis you really had to *want* something to make it work; pain made it hard to concentrate, an excellent – and non-deadly – distraction.

In a way, it was probably better her neck had been broken, because she couldn't feel the agony her body was no doubt suffering. Her headache right now? It was tolerable, although her vision was starting to get a bit spotty.

Not good.

Now that was the understatement of the year.

As Naomi picked the two men up, preparing to dump them out in the woods away from the fight, Monique spun back toward her, her expression furious. Red hot pokers seared into Naomi's mind.

Not again.

Everything went black.

***

The blonde woman collapsed on the forest floor like a puppet who'd had its strings cut. Ari gaped at her. She'd been *floating*. But no matter what creepy, weird thing was going on, she'd been clearly helping, because those two men had stopped whatever they were doing and had collapsed on the ground in agony.

The younger woman – Monique? – stepped toward her. "Look, it's nothing personal, but you have to die."

Sebastian was wavering on his feet as he tried to pick her up, but her wound was already healing. Sweat clung to his face, and his breathing had grown raspy. Was he dying? Could his body fight the liquid silver?

Fear and adrenalin shot through her.

Got to distract her. She shot the redhead a look. "Why?"

"Why what?"

"Why do I have to die?" Ari propped herself on her hands and knees. Gee, her chest still hurt. Maybe that knife had done more damage than she'd imagined. "What did I ever do to you?"

"Exist. You're a hybrid."

"I was born this way, in case you hadn't been told that."

"It's unnatural."

"I'd say it's very natural. Like I said, *born this way*."

Sebastian's voice cut across them. "Did you ever stop to think that maybe she's the next step in evolution?"

"She's an abomination!"

Ari turned to the source of the scream: the older human woman was crawling along the ground, one hand clutching her ribs, which must have been broken from her landing. Her green eyes blazed with anger.

The woman's free fist clenched, and something battered at Ari's mind, trying to break in, to cause the pain that had debilitated her the first time. This time, it didn't work.

Shock froze the human. "Wh-what? How are you doing that?"

Then Monique was in front of her. Ari suddenly threw herself at the younger human, claws bursting from her hands as she sliced at her chest. The redhead fell back with a scream, clutching her torn shirt, before Ari used her speed to launch herself on the older woman, hands locking round her throat.

"Why'd you kill my mother and brother?"

The woman gasped and gurgled, so Ari loosened her grip a little.

"Weres cannot be like us," the choking woman said. "They *must not be* like us. You all had to die."

The strange sensation reached into Ari's mind once more, but again, there was no pain.

"Let her go!" Monique dived at Ari, but Sebastian crash-tackled her to the ground. More than two hundred pounds of enraged were had her pinned, but he was weak, and clearly struggling to hold her down. Ari had to act fast.

"How are you...deflecting me?" Anger tainted the green-eyed woman's features.

Ari looked down. She had hated killing that man, but this woman...she was possessed by hate. It stung Ari like a whip.

"I'm a quick healer. You attacked me, my body healed the wound."

"Impossible."

"I exist, don't I?"

Pain burst through her, and she looked down at her torso. A knife protruded from her flank.

She stabbed me. Again. *Fool me once...*

Without stopping to think, she let her wolf take control. Clawed hands reached out, gripped the human's neck and then twisted. There was a sharp, hard crack, and the woman's body went limp. Within Ari's mind, her wolf howled its victory.

"No!"

Monique struggled, fought to get to the dead woman, but Sebastian held her back. Dirt streaked his face, and leaf litter was in his hair. He'd never looked more impressive.

Ari eyed Monique – her physical resemblance to the dead woman was strong – perhaps they'd been mother and daughter. Ari didn't care. A life for a life. They'd taken two – more, if you counted the pack that had been slaughtered afterwards – so she'd taken two.

She stepped away from the body and pulled the knife from her side, letting it drop to the torn-up ground. There had been enough death: even her wolf agreed.

Taking a deep breath, she met that furious green gaze, and bared her teeth.

"If you want to live, I'd start running."

Chapter Twenty-Five

Naomi was dying.

She had no feeling below her shoulders and breathing was a challenge. Instinct made her call out, but all she could manage was a breathy, "Help!"

This is it. I am going to die here in this forest, alone, and all because I tried to keep a half-breed alive.

When she was younger, she'd been told that if you did a good deed, you'd get rewarded. Well, that was certainly a lie, because all she'd ever tried to do was save people, rather than letting them get murdered by the likes of Monique, and now she was going to die. Worse, Monique and her merry band of hunters had probably killed Subject 2013 and the alpha anyway.

So what had been the point of all this?

She wanted to tell her family that she loved them, but didn't have telepathy, couldn't reach out to her Green-eyed sister, Faith. Maybe Faith would feel her die and come looking for her.

And then the duke and his daughter are going to die...

Faith was not known for her forgiving nature. And she was a stickler for the rules.

One dead sister? Yeah, Faith would lose her mind over that.

Footsteps nearby; they were going to run right by her.

You need to call out. Get help. She opened her mouth, but no sound emerged.

She was going to die, and potentially life-saving assistance was *so* close...

The footsteps stopped. They sounded closer than she'd expected. Opening her eyes, she saw *him*: Parker Ash, the Duke of Ashes. He was staring at her like she'd sprouted a second head, but *he* was there, with blood all over his chin and hands...

He pointed a long, elegant finger at her. "You!"

She wanted to say, "Me," but she didn't have the breath.

Next thing she knew, he was kneeling on the forest floor next to her, his hands touching her everywhere, checking for injuries. It was too bad she couldn't feel a thing; she might have enjoyed it otherwise.

Naomi!

What? She was dying and he *was* ridiculously handsome. Who cared that he was a vampire (aside from her family, who wouldn't know, anyway)? Surely a dead woman got a pass at thinking such a profane thing?

Maybe that just showed how far away from the cause she'd strayed: admiring a vampire, protecting his daughter, saving lives rather than bowing to some twisted sense of justice and taking them.

His hands reached her neck and she gasped.

"What's wrong?" His voice was quiet, deep, and it rumbled through her mind. She could enjoy listening to him speak. Maybe it wouldn't be a bad thing that he'd be the last person she'd ever hear.

She tried to talk, but nothing but air emerged. Licking dry lips and tasting blood, she tried again, "Neck's…broken."

He tilted his head to the side. Show off. "That's a very bad thing, right? For a human?"

She huffed out what might have been a laugh. "Very…bad."

His dark purple gaze locked on her face. "Why are you here? You've been following me."

Surely he couldn't know that. She'd had her sight-shield in place. "Not…you."

His eyes widened. "Aria."

Nodding was beyond her. All she could see was his face now, as if down a long tunnel. It was everything she would have imagined, if she'd ever considered dreaming up the perfect man. Too bad he was a vampire and she was Graced. And that she was dying. "You're pretty."

Had she just said that aloud?

Probably, he was frowning.

"Why were you following my daughter?" At least he had the decency to ignore her outburst.

She swallowed. It hurt. "She…alive?"

"Yes."

"Good."

She shut her eyes. It was time.

Something touched her face.

"Go…away. Dying." Her eyelids flickered open in shock; the duke was rolling up his sleeves, exposing the smooth skin of his forearms.

"I'll Choose you," he said, expression hard. Determined. Like the decision had been made.

"*No!*"

Sure, she was dying now, but she couldn't feel a thing. If he got his blood into her, it might start the healing process, and that would leave her in agony until the third blood transfer. Then she'd die no matter what.

No Graced had ever survived being Chosen, or Bitten.

Ever.

"It's the only way to save you," the duke said, and his stone cold expression softened for a moment, making him unbearably handsome.

"Choose…will…kill me." But the effort of speaking was too much.

The last thing she saw was Parker Ash's face. His cheeks were drawn tight, and his mouth was pursed, almost like he was worried. About her. Which was crazy.

She clawed onto the moment, holding it tight.

Then there was nothing but darkness.

CHAPTER TWENTY-SIX

Sebastian's pulse was weak. He'd collapsed on his back, barely conscious, his head propped up on a broken branch; sweat dripped from his chin, and his shirt and pants were torn to shreds. Somehow, he'd reset his arm, but Ari could tell it wasn't healing like it should.

Monique – the bitch – had run, as fast as she could through the woods. Ari hoped to never see her again.

"Feed him."

Ari spun, ready to face another attacker. Instead, shock glued her to the spot. A stranger stood looking back at her; a stranger who looked like Xave and Nick.

Well, not exactly like them – she just had their coloring – but it was still like a punch to Ari's gut. Gradually, however, the shock wore off. It was good to know that people like her brother could survive, although Ari had no idea how this woman had managed that.

Now was not the time to ask.

"Feed him?" Ari replied at last. "With what?"

"Your blood." The woman moved closer, with a musical tinkling sound. Ari spotted little bells woven into her hair.

"Uh, he isn't a vampire."

"No, but you aren't exactly a normal vampire, either." Her pale gaze narrowed.

Ari raised a hand to her eye. Her eye-patch was on the forest floor somewhere. Then she shook her head. "He's a were. Were's don't drink blood to live."

Sebastian coughed. "Look, I'm not all that into the idea of drinking blood, but I'd do what she says."

"Why?"

His gaze locked on her. "You know what she is, right?"

Blood and pain and death.

Yes, Ari knew what this woman was.

"How is this going to help him?" Ari demanded.

"You drank his blood, yes?"

Ari nodded, fighting the blush that threatened to bloom over her cheeks.

"Then it should work."

"Should?"

The albino gave a half-shrug, with raised palms. "Probably will?"

Ari narrowed her eyes at the albino woman. She didn't like those odds, but still she swiped one of her claws over her wrist, and shoved it at Sebastian. His lips clamped down over the wound and he sucked. The cut was healing too quickly, however, and he bit down on her soft flesh to keep the blood flowing. She hissed at the pain, and he pulled away, guilt stamped on his features.

If this was going to help him… "Do it again," Ari said.

"It hurts you."

"Your kicking the bucket will hurt me. Drink. Now."

When he didn't bite down, she slashed her wrist again and he latched on. Over and over she had to cut herself, until eventually the albino stopped her. Sebastian refused to hurt her again. It would have endeared him to her, expect the constant slashing of her own wrists was frustrating and painful.

The woman looked over Sebastian from head to foot and nodded. "That should be enough."

"What do we do now?" Ari rubbed her wrist. It had healed, but the remembered pain lingered.

"Wait."

"I need some help!" Her father strode into view, carrying a woman over his shoulder – the redhead. The sight of the albino woman didn't surprise him; in fact, he tilted his head at her. "Ralia."

They know each other?

Ari stood up. "Father."

The duke dumped the body at his feet, then closed the distance to his daughter. Carefully, he cupped Ari's cheeks. "You've got blood on you."

She couldn't meet his gaze. "It's okay, I'm healed."

He lowered his hands. "Are you sure?"

"Yes."

Then Sebastian cut through the uneasy discourse, "I thought you told that woman to run."

Ari looked down at Monique's body, the red hair

was stark against the brown earth. "I did."

The duke just shrugged. "She didn't run fast enough."

"But—"

"Look, you can yell at me later for getting rid of this problem," her father slashed a hand through the air, "but I have another issue to take care of."

Lia nodded. "The spy."

Ari frowned. "What spy?"

"Follow me."

He strode back through the forest, to where the strawberry blonde woman lay – the scary one who could fly. Her eyes were shut, and her chest was barely rising from her breathing. Her body was limp, and her skin waxen.

"What's wrong with her?" Ari asked.

"She says she has a broken neck."

Ari frowned. "Could she survive being Chosen?"

Her father looked at her. "You would want to save her? She's been following you."

She had been her stalker?

Ari bit her lip. "She tried to save us just now."

The duke crouched beside the woman.

"I wouldn't do that if I was you." Ralia was at their side in a heartbeat.

"Why not?" Ari asked.

The albino woman shook her head. "She'll die."

"How do you know that?" Ari asked. "Humans usually make the transition."

The woman shrugged, something slightly cagey in her expression. "She's different."

You idiot, Ari thought. *Of course, she's different. Most humans can't throw people around without touching them, and they certainly can't fly.*

"Then she's just going to die?" Something like regret flickered in the duke's eyes.

Ari stared at her father.

Regret?

Did he feel sad at the woman's death?

How does he know her?

What had been going on that she didn't know?

And it's my job to know all these kinds of secrets.

"You do it," Ralia said, her gaze intense as it locked on Ari.

"Me?" Ari had never Chosen or Bitten anyone. She didn't even know if she could – or, as a hybrid, what the outcome would be.

"Ralia…" The duke's voice was low, a warning.

"Aria might be able to succeed."

"But will it hurt?" Ari asked, a little ashamed at the whiny note in her voice.

Ralia flicked her hair over her shoulder. "Afraid of a little pain?"

"I've been beaten black and blue today."

"Then add a few more bruises. She saved your life – are you willing to let her lose hers?"

"But she can't consent." Consent had always been key to Choosing or Biting someone. Becoming immortal wasn't a choice everyone would make, people had the right to make their own decision.

Ralia shrugged. "She's dead if you don't."

Ari's father stood, opening up the space next to the dying woman. "Do it."

Rolling up her sleeve, Ari sighed. "Someone needs

to check on Sebastian."

Ralia nodded. "I'll go."

Ari took the comatose human's hand and bit down. She drank deeply, but couldn't taste any difference in the woman's blood. She was human.

Her father's hand settled briefly on her shoulder. "Enough. Give her your blood now."

Ari slashed her wrist – the left one this time – and placed it over the woman's mouth, angling it so that the blood dripped inside. Crimson droplets trickled from the corners of her lips.

"She's not swallowing."

With a concern Ari rarely saw in him, her father bowed low over the woman. "Drink."

He massaged the human's throat for a few moments. It wasn't working, Ari thought, this savior of hers was going to die. She was about to pull away when cold lips locked over her wrist and the woman swallowed her blood in great, tearing gulps.

"That's it," Ari said. "Keep drinking."

Now, they only had to do this twice more, then wait three days.

Easy.

The only problem was, nothing about this situation had been simple so far.

CHAPTER TWENTY-SEVEN

"How do you feel?" Ari asked. She put the tray of silverware and plates out in the hallway, shutting the door behind her.

Sebastian smiled and waved his spoon in the air. Atrocious table manners, but then, she didn't like him because he knew how to use cutlery. Thankfully.

"Almost as good as new." He was reclining like a king in the large four-poster bed. Thick black curtains hung half-closed, blocking out the early morning sunlight. His bronze skin was still a little pale, but the bounce was back in his manner.

She folded her arms over her chest. "Then why did you request pudding in bed?"

He raised both eyebrows. "Where else would I want to eat pudding?"

A laugh escaped her. Giving up, she climbed up onto the bed and he lifted an arm, so she could snuggle in next to him. "Sure you're okay?"

He rested his chin on the top of her head. "Yes."

Ari wasn't sure how much of it was due to her

blood, but Sebastian had survived the trip back to the estate. It had been touch and go after that. Ralia had drawn as much of the silver out of his system as she could – which had involved a lot of knife work that Ari would prefer not to remember – after which they'd just waited. And waited. And day by day, he'd improved.

According to her father, that much silver should have killed a were Sebastian's age. She was glad his calculations had been proven incorrect.

Sebastian ran his fingers over her braid. "How's Castle?"

"Strange, and I have no idea."

"Still making things move?"

"Just a tad."

The last time Ari had gone to Castle's room to check up on her, everything in the place had been levitating. There had also been minor earthquakes each day since the first blood transfer, all centering on the estate.

Sebastian stroked a hand down her back, then leaned away to pop the spoon on the bedside table. "Did Lia fill you in?"

"On?"

"The Graced."

Ari nodded. "Apparently the damage that Monique and her – Mother? Sister? Aunt? – did to me forced my mind to heal itself. The only way it could do that was create a shield like you've got. So now my mind is hidden from those people and me knowing about them isn't a danger."

Those people.

The Graced.

Even her father hadn't known they existed, but it turned out *he* had a natural mental shield, and so it was safe for him to know about them, too. Well, as much as Ralia – Lia – had been willing to reveal.

What she'd shared had been enough to scare Ari senseless. Those Graced had been afraid of *her?* Heck, she could run fast, and heal quickly, and had super hearing and all kinds of other wonderful abilities, but she couldn't read minds, couldn't move things without touching them or feel other peoples' emotions. Those abilities were frightening. And dangerous.

Ari could understand their need to hide, she did that herself every day, but she wasn't about to murder innocent people in order to keep her secret. A little blackmail was nothing in comparison. However, she couldn't hate them. She wanted to – oh, she wanted to ban every colored-eyed person from coming within a hundred feet of her – but Nick and Xave had been Graced, and she'd loved them more than their own people had.

Their own kind had targeted them for death.

Worse, she'd spent all those years thinking it was something to do with Sebastian. In fact, he'd been the one responsible for their staying alive as long as they had. Somehow his will had kept the mind control at bay and Ari should have been grateful.

She pressed her ear against his chest; the steady thump thump thump of his heart was comforting. She hadn't wanted to lose him, and the black, puckered scars on his chest reminded her of how close she had come to that.

"I'm…sorry I blamed you." Her voice was barely above a whisper.

"What?"

A little louder. "I said I'm…sorry."

He pulled her on top of him, and tugged off her patch so he could look her in the eyes.

"I thought I just heard you say—"

She jabbed him with an elbow.

"Ow!"

"Don't make me repeat it. It burns enough."

"Oh, don't make you repeat the fact that you apologized after years of believing I was a child murderer?" The twinkle in his eyes faded, and he placed a gentle palm against her cheek. "I am sorry, too. That I left, that I wasn't strong enough to stop them from hurting Nick and Layla. I never would have gone if I'd known that was what they were going to do. And I do blame myself for their deaths, even if you don't anymore."

She pressed a kiss against his palm. "If I hadn't been weak, hadn't run…"

"Then you would have died, too. There were so many of them, and they tied up any of the other weres who would have tried to protect you. Plus, you were *ten*."

"But I'm weak. I couldn't save Nick, I couldn't save Xave—"

He put a finger over her lips. "You saved *me*. You saved Castle."

"We don't know about her yet."

"You're a good person, Aria. Stubborn,

pigheaded, obstinate…"

"Those words all mean the same thing."

"Do they? Strange that." He was smiling, and it made her heart beat triple time. He had a dimple! When did he get a dimple? It was sexy.

Think about other things… He didn't need to know she wanted to jump his bones. He was still recovering, and he wasn't like her, so she had to be careful.

"Anyway, what kind of a name is Castle? Do you think it's a nickname?"

"No idea. But you know what?" He placed a hand on the back of her neck, and gently tugged her down, so their lips were almost touching.

"What?"

"You talk too much."

CHAPTER TWENTY-EIGHT

I'm not dead.

Naomi jerked upright and opened her eyes wide. She froze. She'd just sat up – but she had a broken neck, she shouldn't be able to move.

How long have I been asleep?

Maybe she'd fallen into a coma for months, and her body had healed itself. Maybe she hadn't had a broken neck, after all.

Looking around the room, she was startled to see that the furniture – very expensive furniture – was levitating. Quickly diving into her mind, she took several deep breaths, fighting for calm. *Everything is okay. Everything is fine.* You *are fine.*

Opening her eyes again, she took stock of the now-grounded objects.

The room was big enough to hold the entire apartment she'd rented when she moved to Skarva. She was in a wide bed with a beautiful woolen comforter, and there was a metal desk in the far-right corner, accompanied by a beautifully wrought chair.

A small sofa was in the far left corner, near a closed door, and there was a chest at the foot of the bed. Two bedside tables rounded out the room.

She had no idea where she was.

"You're awake."

Flinging herself out of the bed, she landed with a thump on the floor, in a tangle of bed linen. Grunting, she tried to right herself. A hand appeared to help her up, but she ignored it, using her ability to unravel the mess she'd gotten herself into. Then she stood, brushing down her – nightgown? – in a show of dignity.

"Did I startle you?"

That voice.

Her reply died in her mouth. The speaker was even better looking than she remembered – and she didn't know how that was possible – in a super-fine black suit with a dark gray shirt that stretched over broad shoulders. Ash blonde hair, dark purple eyes, and a jaw that looked carved from granite...

It was the Duke of Ashes, in the flesh and up way too close.

Or not close enough?

No.

She was not even going to risk going there.

Memories flooded her: flying through the air, her neck catching on a low-hanging branch, a horrible crunching noise. Using her ability to fly her body back to the fight, breaking those men's arms and legs...the duke threatening to Choose her.

Naomi raised a hand to her throat. "How am I alive?"

The duke stepped back and waved at her, indicating she should return to bed. *Oh no, I don't think so.* She didn't want to be lying down for this conversation. Instead, she walked over to the sofa and sat.

Taking her cue, the duke retrieved the desk chair and sat opposite her, crossing one knee over the other. *He has short hair.* She'd never noticed that before, and it caught her attention. Vampires usually had long hair – it just grew so fast. He would have to cut it every day to keep it that length.

You're losing focus.

And what was that *smell?* Like lemon and spun sugar. It was delicious.

Naomi!

Right. Alive. Questions.

"Well?" She tapped her foot.

"It appears you were Chosen."

"'Appears I was Chosen'?" Naomi frowned. "How is that outcome a surprise to you?"

Hold on.

She was what?

Bolting to her feet, she looked for a bathroom. Somewhere with a mirror.

"Where are you going?"

But she wasn't listening to him. She ran to the door, wrenched it open and coming to a jolting stop. There in the corridor, opposite the door, was a full-length mirror.

"*Mother fucker.*"

The glass shattered.

The duke had his palms raised, as if to calm down a rabid animal. "Look, it will be okay."

She spun on him, and the sound of shattering glass echoed through the hall. "It will *be okay*? How *the fuck* is this okay?"

"Language."

"Oh no, you do *not* get to tell me how to speak." Like a several thousand year old vampire had never heard profanity before, either.

His voice turned placating. "I gather this is a shock…"

"A shock? A *shock*? I shouldn't have survived. I should have died. I was meant to die. And then you, you, you—" She jabbed a finger at his chest. It was like touching smoothly hewn marble. Annoyed at the hint of physical perfection, she jabbed him again.

His hand snaked out too fast for her to follow and grabbed her wrist, stopping her from poking him a third time. "You were meant to die because you are Graced?"

She stopped dead.

How does he know about us?

"Yes," his hand tightened on her wrist, before he stroked a thumb against her racing pulse. "A secret sub-set of humans with special abilities. Ring any bells?"

She tried to tug her arm free, and surprisingly, he let go. "I don't know what you're talking about."

His mouth twisted. "You see, I know you're lying."

"Am not."

"You are."

"I am not a liar." She jabbed him again. How dare he accuse her of lying. And why was his chest so hard with muscle?

"Well, you just employed a falsehood with me. If that's not the definition of a liar, please enlighten me." He crossed his arms over his chest, and glared at her jabbing hand like it was a snake.

He can't possibly know I'm lying. His eyes were dark purple – there wasn't even a speck of Green.

"You made things levitate a lot when you were unconscious. So perhaps you'd like to start over with the truth?"

Her face blanched. She picked up a shard of the mirror to check the damage to her eyes. She looked almost the same, except her hair had gotten really long – which was annoying – and her eyes had changed. They now had starbursts of Gray near her pupil, fading into a dark purple around the rims.

And she still had her ability, that much was obvious.

Whispering, she asked, "How do you know about us?"

"From seeing your compatriots' display, among other things."

"I wasn't working with them."

"Well, that's fortunate."

She frowned.

"They're dead now." His expression was calm as the surface of a lake.

"You killed them?"

"They tried to kill my daughter. What more reason do I need?"

She glared at him, her new eyes slits. "Murder is not the answer!"

"They almost killed you."

I was willing to die.

Actually, that wasn't quite true. She hadn't wanted to die, she'd just come to accept it as the only outcome. She could have fought back early on, prevented herself from getting hurt, but if she'd let loose her power properly, then there wouldn't have been a forest left, or any people in Skarva to save. She would have killed them all.

And now she had to live with this power – her curse – for eternity.

Isn't my luck just great?

CHAPTER TWENTY-NINE

Ari finally found Castle seated at the far end of the sunroom. It was on the third floor of the estate, its huge windows soaring from knee-height to ceiling – now, at night, it was shadowy, lit only by the gas lamps dotted decoratively throughout.

"You're awake," she said.

Castle just stared, her expression shuttered and face cast in darkness. Her long hair was tied back, and she was wearing loose trousers and a pale shirt.

Act calm, Ari thought.

Inside, she was scared. This wasn't just any woman, this was the person that she'd Chosen/Bitten. Chitten? Bisen? Hrm, they were terrible. Maybe she should come up with a new term, like Metamorphosed. Too long. Changed? That was simple enough.

You're getting distracted.

Well, duh. It was better than worrying over the woman she'd Changed and the reaction she was about to get from her. Or not get. The problem was that Castle was powerful and if she wasn't happy with her new situation in life, she could make Ari suffer. A lot.

Could she really hurt us? her wolf asked. *Chosen and Bitten aren't meant to be able to hurt their makers.*

Her wolf had a point, but Castle was Changed. She was different.

Ari was distracted again. It had happened a lot since she'd started the blood transfers. She was jittery now, edgy. Moving forward, Ari held out a hand. "We haven't officially met. I'm Aria Ash."

Castle just sat there. Was she even alive? Maybe Father had lied to her, and the Graced woman had died.

"Hello?" Ari asked.

Castle surged to her feet, and the whole room did a jig. Ari ducked to avoid a flying candelabra, and dodged a metal-framed sofa.

A heartbeat later, everything had settled back in its original place, like all the moveable items hadn't just upped and swirled through the room.

"That's going to take some getting used to," Ari said into the silence.

"Yes, well. Sorry about that." Castle's voice was low and husky. Ari imagined it was better suited a bordello than a drawing room – it was sex on a stick, and the woman wasn't even trying. It was at odds with her country-gentlewoman demeanor. Ari liked incongruity.

Ari waved a hand. "It's fine."

Castle said nothing.

"I get the feeling you're unhappy with me."

The newly Changed woman sighed deeply. "I saved your life and you repaid me with immortality. Most humans would be happy about that, but not me. I'm now stuck."

Bile surged into Ari's mouth. Great. The first – and quite possibly, the only – person she'd ever Changed and they would have preferred to die. Only she'd have luck like that.

"You don't have to…stay alive…if you don't want to." Ari paced the expensive handmade carpet, its yellow and gold metallic fibers catching the gaslight. She couldn't believe they were discussing this. Not after Xave. "I just couldn't have you dying to save me. There'd already been so much death."

"Let me ask you something." Castle sat back down and motioned for Ari to do the same.

Ari took the seat in the adjacent wingback chair. "Go ahead."

"Do you feel any different?"

"Define different." Ari could now change into her wolf, thanks to being mind-raped by that piece of racist scum. She didn't like thinking she had anything to thank that woman for, but breaking the chains of her mind was something. Still, it made her vision haze over to think of how many other people that woman had hurt, and none of them would have had the healing ability Ari did.

She'd recovered. Most wouldn't.

Castle leaned forward, and Ari caught her first proper glimpse of the woman's eyes. She whistled. The center of her irises was a pale Gray, striating out into a deep purple, the same color as Ari's left eye.

She'd never seen anything like them, and might never see their like again.

Touching a finger to the corner of her left eye, Castle let out a sad smile. "I'm a miracle. But not a good one." She shook her head. "So, have you been noticing anything different in your habits – you're hungrier, more tired, restless, you can hear other people's thoughts…?"

"Hah! No on the thoughts. But I've been feeling like I have a lot more energy, energy I can't burn off." And she'd tried, but it made no difference how far or fast she ran. She even left Sebastian for dead, although he claimed it was the poisoning that was making him so slow. Excuses.

"Can you…move anything with your mind?"

Ari shook her head. Then her eyes widened. "You're saying that I could become like you."

"I have no idea. But if you were going to exhibit my ability, you would have already. I wonder." She tapped her chin. "Your father says the worst that happened when I was changing was minor earthquakes and levitation?"

"Yeah." Wasn't that bad enough?

"Hrm."

"That doesn't sound good."

"By rights, if my ability was out of my conscious control during my transformation, this city should be rubble. But it's not." Castle eyed Ari like she was an interesting science project.

"The city? The whole thing?"

Castle nodded. "I could level Skarva without even blinking. But now it's like the pressure is off. It's still there, and I could still do it, but my ability isn't waiting to overflow like it normally does. And suddenly, you have more energy."

"But I haven't gained your ability."

Castle frowned. "No, but that is a good thing, trust me. Maybe you're acting as some kind of well, storing my power."

Ari didn't like the sound of that, either. "Sounds like that could be a problem."

Silence. For quite a long time. At last, Castle met her gaze. "No, I don't think so. In fact, it might actually be a good thing. Time will tell. It would be easier if there had been other Graceds who were Chosen, but as far as I know, I'm the only one."

"Why, because they keep getting killed?" Bitterness seeped into Ari's voice.

"Pretty much. That, and purebloods like me shouldn't be able to make the transition. Maybe your blood, because it's unique, made the difference." Castle rubbed the spot on her wrist where Ari had drunk.

If Ari's freakish bloodlines were responsible for this 'miracle', then it was possible she was unable to Choose a normal person. And if that was the case – and she'd inherited a bunch of crazy energy from Castle – what would she get from other people with different colored eyes?

You know what, I don't want to know.

"So why were you stalking me?" Ari asked. "You were pretty good, by the way."

A sigh. "I had heard rumors there might have been a Graced vampire in Skarva."

Ari blanched.

"Not you. The Duchess of Ravens' daughter. Then I spotted you with your eye-patch, and saw how you moved...I thought you might have heterochromia, but instead of a yellow eye, I thought it might be Gray. I had no idea you were half were. Not until Monique came to town."

"If you'd known, what would you have done?"

"I've already spoken to your father about this."

Ari frowned. "I am not my father."

"A truer statement I've never heard." Castle's hand made a fist. "You want the truth? I would have done nothing. Not unless you were proving dangerous, and in the whole time I followed you, you never hurt anyone, apart from stealing their secrets. Although there was Vince, but I figure being shot in the chest with an arrow warranted a similar response."

Ari linked her fingers together. "I don't know what you're talking about."

A small smile danced on the corner of Castle's mouth. "I'm sure you don't."

"I guess that means you're not like other Graced," Ari said.

"Most Graced don't care about anything apart from living their lives and keeping their identities a secret. But I am from a family of Hunters, and they kill what they fear. I just never believed in letting blind hatred rule my emotions. So I handle 'justice' my own way."

Man, Castle was still scary. At least Ari knew she was compassionate, though, and that meant a lot.

Those unique eyes flashed. "And it's Naomi, by the way."

"Naomi?"

Castle held out a hand. "Hi Aria, my name is Naomi. It is nice to meet you."

CHAPTER THIRTY

Sebastian shoved the last of his clothing into his backpack and sat on the edge of the bed. Time to leave the Grumpy Bear, but what should he do next? Go and say goodbye to Ari, beg her to let him stay with her, or get moving and be gone by sundown?

Tough choices, because he didn't want to do either.

He couldn't stay here in Skarva, pretending to not care about her. Sure, he'd only been with her a couple of weeks, but it didn't matter.

"She doesn't smell like your mate."

Sebastian whirled, snarling at the intruder. Lia stood in the doorway. "I said, she doesn't smell like your mate."

"So? That whole thing is rubbish."

"It isn't."

"You really believe that?"

She stopped in front of him; her hair had orange stripes in it today. "Your ancestry goes back over ten generations. Most weres with that kind of lineage have a Graced or two in their background. The psychic sense of smell is a real thing, but all it does is tell you that the person is a good match. You don't magically fall in love and live happily ever after. It just makes it a bit easier, I guess."

"So what if Aria doesn't smell like whatever it is mates smell like. It doesn't matter."

"Really? So if a woman walked by with the most irresistible scent you've ever come across, you wouldn't leave Aria for her?"

No.

The response was immediate and instinctual. He didn't care about anyone else, had never reacted with his whole being toward another person the way he did with Aria. She taunted him, maddened him, aroused him, and challenged him. There'd never be another person like her.

He eyed Lia. "What generation wolf are you?"

"This isn't about me."

"Come on."

A dark shadow flitted across her expression. "Third on my father's side. Second on my mother's."

Wait – her mother had been *first generation*? His mouth dropped. "How old are you?"

"Now that one I am not going to answer."

"Fine." It was pretty clear he was a mere pup in comparison.

"But you never answered me." She twirled a braided piece of hair around a pale finger.

"No, it wouldn't matter to me. I wouldn't leave her for some future maybe. Why would I want to? She's perfect."

Well, perfect for him.

"That is the correct answer." With that Lia retreated from the room, shutting the door behind her.

A thud and then a snarl. "If I am so perfect, then why are your bags packed?"

Sebastian glanced over his shoulder. There was Ari, just inside the window, wearing that familiar blue cloak. Her hood was thrown back, her entire body giving off a challenge.

"I didn't think you wanted me to stay."

She flicked her braid over her shoulder. "What kind of an idiot are you?"

He decided no response was probably the best response.

She stepped forward and poked him in the arm. It hurt. Her fingers were pointy. "I trusted you." Poke. "I let myself believe in you." Poke. "I *saved your life.*" Poke. He was going to be covered in bruises. "I *cared* about you. And now you're going to leave without even saying goodbye?"

He held up both hands. "I was going to say goodbye."

"Lia's note says otherwise."

Why, that meddling —

"Well, there was a fifty per cent chance I was going to say goodbye. I thought you might not want to see me again."

"Why would you think a stupid thing like that?"

"Because you have your wolf. You can change. You avenged your brothers' and mother's death."

"So?" She ripped off her eye-patch.

"So, what?"

"Yes, I have all those things. But what good are they if you're gone, too? I can't keep losing the people I care about. I *can't*."

His throat seized up, but his body knew what to do. He enfolded her in a hug so tight he was crushing her. Her arms wrapped around him and she squeezed him back. "I thought you wouldn't want this anymore."

She tilted her chin up. "Are you crazy? We have a small thing called 'chemistry'."

"Lia says you aren't my mate. Because I can't smell you."

"No one can smell me." Her expression grew sad. However, a smile bloomed slowly. "But I can smell you. And you smell amazing."

"Really? What do I smell like?" It had to be something manly. Like leather. Cologne. Apples. Although he had no idea why apples were a manly fruit. Whatever.

"I'm not telling."

"Tell me."

"No."

"Tell me."

Did that mean he was *her* mate, if she could smell him and it was amazing?

"No." She kissed him, and he forgot what he was asking. When she pulled away, it was with a small nibble. "So. Are you going to move in with me, or what?"

"What will your father say?"

"It's a big estate, he probably won't even notice."

"I don't believe that."

"Fine. He says you're welcome, and if you break my heart, he'll break you. Although he did add that he believes he'd have to break what's left of you, because I would have already taken care of business."

"He said all that?"

"Yes, he was feeling chatty." Her tone lacked the usual venom.

"Everything okay with you and your father then?"

"I think I understand him a bit better now. I still hate what he did to Xave, but I get it. Changing Castle has given me a bit of an idea." She rubbed a cheek, almost rueful.

"Wait, did I just hear you say you were wrong?" He backed away.

"No!"

"I think I heard that." He darted for the door, but didn't make it. A second later he was shoved up against the wooden panel, and Aria was pressed right up against *him*. He hardened instantly.

"Do I have to move my stuff right now?"

She bit his chin.

"Ow."

"Maybe not right now."

And then her lips were on his.

"I love you."

She paused. "Good."

"Nothing to say back?"

"Not right now."

The minx.

Then she was dragging his head down and kissing him. Suddenly, his mouth bloomed with the taste of frozen strawberries dipped in sugar. It drove him crazy.

Maybe we are mates, after all.

Then she did something wicked with her tongue, and he was lost.

EPILOGUE

Naomi was a dead woman walking.

Once her family found out she was alive, they'd come looking. If they came, Hunters would follow, and Naomi's eyes were a dead giveaway as to what she'd become.

It was strange. A few days ago, she would have welcomed the wooden stake, but not anymore. Her power, still great, was no longer a yawning chasm at her feet. With part of it being siphoned off into Aria, for the first time in her life, she could breathe.

She opened the door to Parker Ash's office with her mind, and then shut it behind her the same way. She strolled casually up to his desk and took a seat opposite the duke. "You asked to speak with me?"

She refrained from looking at him directly; he was still too handsome for his own good, and her body had a habit of reacting to it, which she didn't like. He was a vampire. He would be able to...smell it.

So are you.

Yeah, but that wouldn't make it any less

embarrassing.

The duke lowered his pen, and pushed aside his pile of paperwork. "Yes, I did request your presence. An hour ago."

"I was busy." She wasn't lying, but she'd been busy ignoring him. For her own sanity.

Both of his eyebrows rose, just slightly. "I thought we should discuss what was found in your apartment."

Naomi forced a smile. "I'm sure it was rather boring reading."

"Yes, considering it was all in code, which I am still in the process of cracking. I'm about halfway there."

"I wouldn't bother. It's all pretty dull. Financial reports."

"You know, I can tell when you lie. It's off-putting, so please stop."

She wondered how he managed to do that, but she wasn't going to think too hard about it. The less she thought about Parker Ash, the better.

"Can I have my books back?"

"No."

"Why not?"

"Because I have a feeling they detail the results of your spying, and I don't want people finding out about Aria. Is that sufficient reason?"

While it gutted her that she'd never get back all those meticulous records, she could see his point. She'd just have to hunt them down, later. They were *hers*, after all.

"Well?"

"Oh, I didn't realize you were actually asking a question. Yes, it's sufficient."

He tapped a finger on the ink blotter on his desk. "I'm glad to hear it. Now, the other reason I asked you here. I may have sent a note to your family. I found their address in your correspondence."

"*What*?" She burst out of her chair, and everything in the room jumped with her.

Parker shoved himself back from the desk, probably to avoid having the heavy metal furniture land on his foot. "That is going to take some getting used to." He eyed the floating furniture pieces like they were strange insects that had crawled onto his lap.

"I won't be sticking around for you to get used to it." Now her family had been alerted to her situation...

"Where would you go? You need to stay with your Chooser."

"Changer." She re-settled the furniture where it belonged.

"Excuse me?"

"Aria has decided that she Changed me, rather than Chose or Bit." Naomi didn't really care what it was called, she just wanted to annoy the duke.

"I see."

He probably did.

"Fine," he sat down at his desk. "You need to stay with your Changer – especially considering your...ability."

"But if I stay here, everyone is in danger."

"From you?"

"From my family."

The duke frowned. "Oh, I see. Well, that's the part I haven't told you." He coughed into his hand. "I may have written to them and said you died in a fight, while trying to save my – young – daughter from harm."

Naomi blinked. "You said what?"

"That you were dead."

"You *lied*."

"You *could* have died."

"*You lied*." She fought a smile. Mr.-I-am-so-into-honesty had fibbed. And what a fib.

"Well, I couldn't have more of your kind coming here."

Her amusement died. "My kind?"

"I saw what they did to Aria and Sebastian, and I saw what they did to *you*. You are one of them. If they could kill you now, what would they do to you later? Family or not, I was not inviting them here."

Wait – he was *protecting* her?

Protecting Aria. She Changed you, and now you're her responsibility. And you're psychically linked to her. Naomi dying could cause massive mental trauma to Aria. Who'd probably heal, to be fair, but it wouldn't be pleasant.

"I hope you won't be angry, but I can't let you contact your family, either. They have to believe you're dead."

"They'll come here anyway. They won't believe I'm gone until they see the body."

"I may have mentioned I'd had your remains cremated in the vampire tradition."

Wow, he'd been on a roll.

"They will still be suspicious. Grays of my...strength...don't usually go down without a fight." Or half a city.

"Then they can come and visit. But we will deal with it at the time."

My family think I'm dead. Her heart broke at how Marcia would feel upon reading that letter. Her sister was a Blue, and had always felt too deeply. Petra would be sad, but they'd never really been close – mostly because Naomi had been too afraid of hurting her non-Graced sister. And Fin, well, she hadn't seen him for a decade. He wouldn't even know.

That left Faith.

Faith was the deadliest of the lot. Naomi just had to hope that the letter would take a really, really long time to find her.

She'd miss her siblings, oh, how she'd miss them, but she had a new life here. A new beginning. What's more, if they knew about her, they'd probably try and protect her – maybe even Faith would, too – and that would put them in danger. Because Parker Ash was not a vampire to be messed with, and neither was his daughter.

Her power was no longer overwhelming. Her mind was unburdened, and her neck was repaired. Meeting the duke's stare, she gave a small, rare smile. "Basically then, I'm free."

Ash's expression lightened, and he reached across the desk, taking one of her hands in his. His skin felt cool, smooth, and surprisingly reassuring. His fingers tightened against hers. "You're free."

ACKNOWLEDGMENTS

Thank you to everyone who has helped support me this year during my mad dash to get four new books out. And a special thanks goes out to the other authors who were part of the *Venom and Vampires* boxed set. Together, we made the USA Today Bestselling List – and *Ashes* was part of that collection.

Specifically, I also want to thank my wonderful beta reader Joanne Danton and my editor supreme, Pete Kempshall. *Ashes* is a small story, but one that continues to share glimpses of the strange, terrible, and sometimes wonderful world of the Graced. I hope you enjoyed it!

Amanda Pillar is a USA Today Bestselling author and award-winning editor who lives in Victoria, Australia, with her husband and two cats.

Amanda is the author of the Graced series, the Tangled Threads Series, and co-author of the Moonlit Hills series. She has also had numerous short stories published. She has co-edited six fiction anthologies and solo-edited two: *Bloodstones* and *Bloodlines*, published by Ticonderoga Publications.

In her day job, she works as an archaeologist.